The Origins of Constantine

An Intern Diaries Novella

D. C. Gomez

GOMEZ EXPEDITIONS

Cover design by Christine Gerardi Designs

Edited by Cassandra Fear

Proofread by Michelle Hoffman

ISBN: 978-1-7321369-4-6 for Paperback Editions

Published by Gomez Expeditions

Request to publish work from this book should be sent to: author@dcgomez-author.com

For every person who has a "furry" companion and has discovered
unconditional love through them:
this book is for you.

Chapter One

P resent day- Texarkana, TX
It was strange to have snow on the ground in Texarkana. Even in early February, the coldest of the winter months for the area, snow was rare. The twin cities of Texarkana—one in Texas and one in Arkansas—normally only got one snowfall per season. If this was their designated day, it was a sad day for the kids. Barely an inch had fallen, and the only remaining flakes were on dead grass.

It was Friday night, and Constantine sat in the passenger's seat of Bob's 1980 Toyota Truck, staring out the window and looking completely lost in thought.

"Boss, are you okay?" Bob asked Constantine as he parked the truck in the empty lot next to Sonic on New Boston Road.

"You know, it's just not fair. I have been around longer than that stupid franchise." Constantine let out a growl as he spoke, not meeting Bob's eyes. "How dare they sue me? I could buy that whole thing and then destroy it." His feline eyes dilated in anger.

If anybody else would have told Bob they were going to buy a major TV/movie franchise just to destroy it, Bob would have laughed. But this was Constantine, who had more money than God. He was also a five-thousand-year-old talking cat who was the right-hand-man of Death, and also the guardian/trainer of all the Interns that worked for Death. If Constantine wanted something or someone gone, he could make it happen.

"Boss, you made a YouTube video taunting them," Bob told Constantine, keeping his voice low and flat. The last thing Bob wanted was Constantine angry with him.

"Small technicalities," Constantine replied, waving his paw in the air in a dismissive gesture.

"Your video went viral and you dared them to dispute your claim that your Camaro was the real Bumblebee," Bob added as he pulled a bowl from his glove compartment.

Constantine went quiet, staring at Bob with a hard look, which made Bob squirm in his seat.

Bob was in his forties, an Army Veteran with sandy-blond hair, and a man with a new lease on life. When he was kidnapped last fall by a bunch of volatile witches, they almost sacrificed him, but his friend Isis Black saved him before they got the chance. Right after, Bob learned that Isis took the job as Death's North American Intern to save him. After that, he vowed he would always protect her. Granted, Isis was one tough cookie. As a former soldier herself, she was slowly becoming a force to be reckoned with. She was also a talented musician and the sweetest person in town. With her mocha complexion, silky black hair, and sparkling eyes, she was easy to look at, too.

For many years, Bob had thought he was insane. The things he had seen in the war had destroyed his self-esteem and his sense of reality. After his rescue from the witches, he felt validated and vindicated. He wasn't crazy; the world was just a lot more complicated than he had imagined. So, when he was offered a job working for Death, he jumped on the opportunity. He could keep an eye on Isis, but also do some good for others. He finally had a stable income—a huge one for that matter—and he was no longer homeless. The fact that right now he was pouring a milkshake in a bowl for a cat that talked was just another day in paradise for Bob.

"Here you go, Boss." Bob put Constantine's bowl in front of him and watched as the cat sipped his shake. Bob wasn't crazy about fast food. He preferred to cook, but milkshakes were a weakness he shared with Constantine. Especially Sonic's shakes.

"You know they add something to their shakes to make them so addictive. These are not normal," Constantine told Bob as he licked his shake.

"I agree, but does it matter? They are so good," Bob told Constantine as he slurped his shake and watched the cars drive by. It was a slow Friday night in town, but it was still early, so it wouldn't be long before the teenagers were out driving around.

"Death told me to leave it alone," Constantine said so softly Bob almost missed it.

"What happened?" Bob asked.

"Death said I couldn't retaliate and to change the name." Constantine's eyes were misty and his lower lip trembled. "I can't give him another name. He is going to be the only nameless one."

Bob wanted to reach over and pet his boss, but was afraid of losing his hand. Constantine might look like a Maine Coon, but Bob knew he was anything but helpless.

"Boss, you should do like Prince." Bob almost jumped out of his seat with excitement.

Constantine raised an eyebrow. "Go on. Explain."

"Name him a symbol and then just call him the Camaro formerly known as Bumblebee or the Camaro for short," Bob told him with a huge grim.

"My man, I like that," Constantine replied, tapping his face with his claws. "Now we just need a symbol. I got it, we will go hieroglyphics and still call him Bumblebee. Just don't tell Isis," he finished with a diabolical smile.

"You still know how to write hieroglyphics?" Bob knew Constantine was from ancient Egypt, but he didn't know much else about the cat's past.

"You never forget your first love, or your homeland," Constantine answered in a purr.

Bob's phone went off, and the sound surprised him. It was new, and he wasn't used to having so many gadgets, but Bartholomew made sure he had the latest in everything. Bartholomew was the team's boy genius. At eleven years old, the kid could do miracles.

Not to mention, Bob was sure he was an international arms dealer on top of a hacker.

Reaching to his dashboard, Bob tapped his icon for phone and put it on speaker. "Isis, what's going on?" Bob said in greeting. His caller ID had shown Isis's smiling face.

"Please tell me you guys are having more luck than me." Her voice sounded strained over the phone.

"We got a mocha Java chiller from Sonic. Does that count?" Constantine asked as he licked his shake.

"You guys are having shakes while I freeze to death out here?" Isis whined.

"Why are you not inside the mini?" Bob asked Isis. After the witches blew up her minivan last fall, Constantine gave Isis a midnight-blue mini-Cooper, which she absolutely loved.

"I'm trying to get the drop on him," Isis said, this time lowering her voice.

"Girl!" Constantine told Isis, almost growling. "Get your skinny butt in that car and stop being silly!" He shook his head.

Bob stifled his laugh.

"You told me to be resourceful," Isis told him, back to whining.

"Yes, I did, but we are tracking a soul that was killed by a truck while running naked." Constantine covered his face with his paws. "You are not going to sneak up to him. That man was faster than an Olympic runner. Get in your car and start cruising around."

"What are you two going to do, besides snack?" Isis sounded like a kid who just had her ice cream cone stolen. For a young lady in her twenties, she sure could act like a child at times.

"We are watching New Boston Road, so when he comes down this way like the naked comet he is, we will follow him," Constantine said.

Bob gave Constantine a weary look.

"Fine," Isis told them in a defeated tone. "But if you see him, call me."

"Of course," Constantine told her and disconnected the call.

"She hates when you do that," Bob told Constantine as he stared at the dash on the truck.

Constantine grinned. "I know, but it is hard to have the last word if you are still on the line," he said before diving back in to his shake.

"Boss, how exactly am I going to be of any help here?" Bob asked after a minute of silence. "I can't see the dead like Isis can." That was one of the gifts Death gave to her Interns. At times, Bob was grateful he didn't get the gift. Unfortunately, on work nights when they were on stake-outs, the lack of magic could be a hindrance.

"Oh, you will be a lot of help since I'm right here," Constantine said, not even looking at Bob. Bob stared at Constantine, his mouth hanging open. "Close your mouth before you swallow a fly."

"I'm confused," Bob slowly admitted.

"You don't think the only thing I got from Death was long life, do you?" Constantine said with a wink.

"As long as I'm around you, you will get to see the supernatural world with the rest of us. Sometimes it's not as pretty as people think." Constantine finished his milkshake and smiled at Bob.

Bob tossed the bowl in his cupholder so he wouldn't forget to take it in when they got back to Reapers. He didn't want to think about what it might smell like in a week if he forgot it.

"Boss, I have been wondering, how did you meet Death?" Bob asked, fidgeting with his straw. "If that's too personal, you don't need to answer."

"That's a unique question. Nobody ever wants to know my origins. Normally, after Interns agree to take the job, they only care about getting paid, and their fringe benefits of course." Constantine licked his paw and wiped it across his face, then got comfortable in his seat.

"Well, I kind of know how Interns get hired, and it doesn't make any sense to me," Bob explained.

"It's a little unconventional, but we need people with a moral compass, not just skills and abilities." Constantine said. "After our Intern from hell, we started to look if the person we hired would feel any guilt, remorse, or a sense of responsibility if they killed another human being. We really wanted to know if they would care for the wellbeing of the souls. Hence the reason Isis is perfect for the job. She cares about everyone."

"If you say so." Bob gave Constantine a sideways glance. "But how about you? How did you started working for Death?"

Constantine didn't say anything for a few minutes, and Bob thought he might not answer, but then he did. "It was a different era and a very different place. I grew up in Memphis, the first capital of the United Kingdom of Egypt back in 3100 BC. It was the pride of Menes, the king who united Upper and Lower Egypt." Constantine's voice had become silky smooth and everything sounded like a soft purr.

"I thought Egypt had pharaohs?" Bob asked Constantine.

"Pharaohs is a Greek word. In Egypt, we called them kings and queens, just like everyone else. Granted, the word pharaoh has a bit more mystique so it kind of stuck." Constantine rolled his eyes. "But Memphis was marvelous, like nothing you had ever seen. Temples were works of art. Gods were worshipped and their likeness glorified for all time. Not like today, where people have one God and they can't even talk about him in public. Feel bad for JC."

Bob bit his lip so he wouldn't laugh. Only Constantine would call Jesus "JC."

"Do you miss it?" Bob asked quietly, hoping he wasn't prying too much.

"Those were different times. I enjoy the conveniences of this modern era. But humanity lost a little of its wonder in its development." Constantine's eyes were glued out the window. "Memphis was located south of the delta, near the Nile. Most people only think of Egypt as a desert, but that was not the case back then. The grounds near the delta were fertile, and palm trees were everywhere. The city itself was beautiful, and even the poor areas had their charms. Stone houses and temples were everywhere. Some can still be found today if you know where to look," he said, and Bob could see the reflection of Constantine's smile through the window.

"Sounds incredible," Bob told Constantine.

"Do you really want to know how I met Death?" Constantine asked Bob, meeting his eyes.

"If you don't mind telling me, then yes," Bob said, not looking away.

"Okay, I'm sure we have the time. I'm not expecting our streaker to swing by anytime soon." Constantine took his favorite pose of the Sphinx and Bob leaned on his door, getting comfortable.

"Death has been around since the beginning of time. He has had many different forms and more than one identity. Back when I met him, he was a lot different. He was still taking care of the dead, but he was known as Anubis." Constantine slowly looked at Bob after he was finished.

Bob's mouth was wide open in shock.

Chapter Two

Around 3140 BC- Hiku-Ptah (commonly known as Memphis, Egypt)

Dawn was quickly approaching and the little cat limped down the stone street. He'd barely escaped the night before. According to humans, cats were worshipped in the Hiku-Ptah, or was it Inbu-Hedj. Humans kept changing the name of the great city. He liked the new one better. It was more accurate since it meant "White Walls," and the palace was famous for its white walls that shone like a beacon in the day. That was the place where cats were truly worshipped—in the palace. If you were a palace cat, your life was a dream. For the rest of the city cats, it was survival of the fittest.

The little cat knew all too well about survival. He had made it to adulthood on his own, fighting his way across the city. The marketplace had its clan and no outsider was welcome. The little cat knew it wasn't fair, but it was the only place always booming with people and food, so he did what he had to do. Based on the conversations of the humans, Inbu-Hedj was the metropolis of the world. The little cat had no idea what that meant, but he thought it might have to do with the strangers who always came to buy and sell things. Unfortunately, the market clan wouldn't share, and too many times he got in a scuffle with the Alpha.

The temple of Ptah had a clan and those stupid priests kept them well fed. The weird looking cats there were so fat they couldn't move. Of course, they had no trouble hiring their dirty work to the plaza clan.

Everyone had a clan. Except him. He refused to bow down to any other cat, so every night, he fought. Normally, he found refuge with the kids in the working area of the city. They barely had enough food for themselves, but the little they had they shared. He hated to bother them, though. They had enough trouble keeping up with the construction crew with the few supplies they did have.

Last night had been the worst. He was beat up by three disciplinarians. The little cat was only ten pounds, but it was solid muscle. He was fast, too. His claws were sharp and the stripes down his body were bright because he took good care of himself. In fact, his grooming habits were impressive. Even though the fight hadn't been his, he couldn't help but jump in. He hated to see the weak get hurt. The disciplinarians were going to make an example out of a kitten. He knew they would kill him, and all for a piece of fruit. The poor kitten was starving, but nobody cared. The beating had been rough, but he managed to get the kitten and himself out alive.

The little cat had to drag the kitten down to the working-class section of town. It took all night since he had to avoid the clans roaming the streets. He finally made it and left him with one of the working kids.

Ammon was the head of his house, and the little cat felt bad for him because of it. His father had died in a construction accident while building the great White Walls, and now Ammon had to work to take care of his mom and sister. Even with the little food they had, they were always good to the little cat. They took in the kitten and hid him.

It was time for the little cat to disappear for a while. Interfering with punishments and laws was a crime the clans took very seriously. On a normal day, he would have lounged around the statues of King Menes and sunbathed. Today, he needed to catch the workers heading to Saqqara, the necropolis of Inbu-Hedj. He loved Saqqara, though. It was clean, quiet, and deserted. Only the ancient priest and artisans were ever there, and the strange man with the funny head. The little cat enjoyed watching him, too. He was different, even smelled different. Not fully human, but not animal, either.

The little cat made his way out of the city as quickly as his beat-down body would take him. If he missed the crew, it would take him too many sun ups to make the trip alone. He would probably never make it. The area around Saqqara was guarded by wild beasts. The little cat had no intentions of becoming dinner to anyone today, so he hurried.

The workers would be arriving soon to the Saqqara and Anpu wandered the halls of the newly built temple. It was a beautiful structure with a large, circular room in the middle for the preparation of the dead. It had adjacent chambers to house all the priests and their equipment. Like everything else King Menes built, it was a wonder in itself. After uniting lower and upper Egypt, his first plan was to make the new monarchy something to be marveled at.

Why did he have to dedicate to that old fool of Ptah? Anpu wondered.

As he walked the corridors, he realized how much he hated the name Anpu. He was sticking to his favorite version, Anubis. It wasn't like anyone was going to complain. Not when he spent his days alone.

"Even that annoying cow-god had more followers than me," Anubis told himself out loud. "When I find Isis, I'm going to strangle the life out of her." Anubis kicked at the stones in the chamber, sending them flying into the air. "'This is a great opportunity,' she said. 'You will be adored' she said. 'Manage the dead,' she said." Anubis imitated her high-pitched voice. He slammed his fist against a wall and slowly kept walking.

Isis had been right, though. He had seen to all the dead, watching over their burials and looking after them. People had brought treasures to his feet, but nobody ever stayed. Even the vermin avoided him when he got near. His priests were so old, Anubis was sure he would be burying them shortly. They never noticed his presence, and the few times he spoke to them, they scattered. Then he didn't see them for days.

It wasn't fair. All the other gods had cults and people. He had the dead, but not for very long because Osiris took them after their judgment.

Anubis was afraid of spending his eternity alone and soon forgotten.

When the workers arrived, Anubis strolled in their direction. Menes had decided to expand Saqqara, something Anubis appreciated. The new people in the necropolis provided a form of entertainment, since nothing new ever went on around him. Anubis wasn't sure why, but the crew always had a pair of foremen that looked like they needed a haircut. Even for the strange custom of the times, the pair looked more like wild dogs than humans. They even preyed on the weak and tormented the others. Anubis shook his head. He couldn't even find competent people for the construction of the city.

From the door of the temple, Anubis watched the workers load up supplies, food, and materials for the necropolis. He couldn't figure out why they didn't name the stupid place after him. He was the only god that ever went there.

After a few minutes watching, he got bored. As he turned to leave, he saw a little cat climbing out of one of the chariots. It was the same cat Anubis had seen before, and he'd never paid him any attention. Except he was the only animal who ever came to Saqqara, so maybe he should have.

There was something different about him today, though. He was limping. Before Anubis could analyze the situation any further, the little cat disappeared into the crowd.

Anubis went back to wandering the temple halls. The everyday inventory of supplies bored him to death. He could leave Saqqara and see the world at any moment, but he had already been everywhere there was to see. Plus, he was tired of seeing it alone. None of the other gods ever visited. Why would they? They were all too busy being worshipped and having parties.

Anubis was deep in his misery when he stumbled on the little cat sitting by the main window of the temple. This was Anubis's favorite location because he could see the outside world and the working chamber all at once.

"Hey there, Cat, you are in my spot," Anubis told the cat, and even to him it sounded like he was growling. No wonder the sound of his voice always made people run away.

The little cat didn't run away. Instead, he slowly stretched, then one paw at a time, he made his way over to Anubis. For a minute, he had no idea what the cat might do, and it made nerves jitter inside him, at least until the cat met his eyes and rubbed against his leg.

Anubis didn't know what to do, so he backed up a few inches and looked down at the feline. "Can you see me?"

"Meow," the little cat replied.

"Are you a spy for Bastet?" Anubis crossed his arms over his chest and narrowed his eyes.

The little cat tilted his head to the right and stared at Anubis once more.

"Don't give me that look," Anubis told the cat. "She claims all the felines are her property. Crazy banshee."

Anubis wasn't sure what to do. The little cat wasn't running away. In fact, he wasn't even moving. It felt like a lifetime ago since he had last talked to anyone.

With a glance up and down the corridors, Anubis realized nobody was coming. As usual. "What do I have to lose?" Anubis told the cat as he sat down on the floor next to him.

The little cat made his way slowly towards Anubis and took a seat next to him. They were both sitting on the ground, leaning back and staring at the empty hallways. The feeling was very different. It was still silent, but he was no longer alone. He kind of liked it, so he smiled.

"Okay, little fellow, what's your name?" Anubis asked the little cat. In turn, the cat just looked back at him. "You don't have a name?"

"Meow," replied the little cat.

"We need a better form of communication," Anubis joked, rubbing his head. "Let's start with problem number one: you need a name. I can't be calling you Cat all the time, and I have a feeling you are not going away."

"Meow," the little cat said again.

"That's what I figured," Anubis said, looking down at the stubborn cat. "How about Constantine?"

The little cat's ears perked up and his eyes got really big.

Anubis chuckled at the cat's excitement. "I think you like it."

"Meow," replied the little cat, this time purring and rubbing on Anubis.

"Hey, watch it. No drooling on the god," Anubis told Constantine while he rubbed his head again. "I heard the name in my travels. It's strong and defiant, just like you. You can call me Anubis." He stroked Constantine's back.

Constantine made a loud noise at the touch, then his body trembled. When Anubis picked him up, Constantine squirmed in his arms. His body started trembling.

Closing his eyes, Anubis passed a soft hand over Constantine's body. "I really hope the other guy is in worse shape than you. You took one big beating, my little Constantine." Anubis inspected Constantine as he spoke. "Stay still, boy; this will only take a moment."

Very gently, Anubis rubbed Constantine's sides. He placed the little cat down and watched him carefully. Constantine moved one paw first and then a second one. Anubis watched as the little cat moved without flinching or limping. Confirming his theory, Constantine leaped in the air and bounced off his paws.

"Slow down, now. I know you are feeling better, but healing takes a lot out of you," Anubis told Constantine. The cat swayed towards Anubis, his tail and head straight up and his eyes shining with... something. Was it happiness? It had been so long since he'd seen that emotion that he wasn't sure. "You should eat and rest, you will need it to heal completely."

Constantine had just sat down next to Anubis, but at the mention of the word food, his head snapped up and his eyes roamed the area.

Anubis laughed. "I thought cats were worshipped in the city? That's what the crazy Bastet tells me," Anubis said in a mocking voice. "Here let me fix that." He snapped his fingers and a large plate of meat appeared, and next to it was a bowl of milk.

Constantine's tongue fell out of the side of his mouth. After a quick glance at the plate, he met Anubis's eyes. "It's all yours, Constantine. I'm not sure why humans keep bringing me food. Like I eat that stuff," Anubis told Constantine, who was already devouring the meal. "Just do me a favor and don't tell anyone I healed you. It won't look good that the god of death is now curing the living. Besides, I think there's some weird rule about not getting involved with humans and the living."

"Meooo," Constantine replied around a mouth full of food.

"I'll take that as a yes," Anubis told Constantine. He leaned back and watched the little cat as he purred over his food.

Anubis had no need to eat, but he understood the feeling of hunger. He looked down at his new little friend. He had wanted a companion more than anything, although he hadn't expected it to come in such a small package with no vocabulary.

Chapter Three

C onstantine had been sleeping on and off for several days. He found out his new friend's name was Anubis and he was a god. Constantine had never met a god before. Inbu-Hedj was packed with images of gods, and people would kneel before the images to pray. Gods meant nothing to Constantine, though. None of them have ever helped him. Until now. In fact, his body felt better than ever. There were no injuries marring it any longer, and for the first time in his life, his belly was truly full. Anubis gave it all without asking for anything in return. Constantine had never met anyone like him.

Anubis had told Constantine many stories of exotic places and strange people. None of it made any sense to Constantine, but it excited him to hear about it. It was also the first time in his life he didn't have to hunt for food or fight for his life. Anubis had told him to start walking around on the third night.

"Constantine, your muscles will need movement. I promise after you do it, you'll feel so much better," he had said.

Constantine had no idea how Anubis knew so much, but he followed his orders.

Normally, Constantine would spend his days in Saqqara hunting for rodents and spying on the priest. With his food problem resolved, however, he had the time to actually spy on everyone else, so he strayed through the new temple, examining all the rooms. Since the last time he had been there, the artisans had added an additional room—a treasure room. It was packed with jewels and fine cloths, but the doors were left wide open, which meant it wasn't very secure. Anubis had told Constantine some of the items inside would help set up his temple, which made him beam with joy. The rest of the stuff would be for the burial of a royal.

For some reason, humans also liked to bury their dead with food, which made no sense to Constantine. The humans smelled more than dead, so what use would they have for food? And since they didn't need it, he decided it shouldn't go to waste. He began taste testing everything, and he was so busy doing it that he never noticed the two men who entered the room. As he took a bite of fish, he finally heard them. His ears shot straight up and he crawled towards them. He instantly recognized them as the foremen of artisans, and he didn't like either one of them.

The two men carried sacks with them, and the shorter one pointed at different items while the taller one grabbed the items that were pointed to, and then some. Constantine's heart dropped when he realized they were stealing all of Anubis's temple ornaments, and that would devastate him. He didn't ask for much, but he really wanted a temple.

"Are you sure nobody is going to find out?" the tall one asked in a slurred voice.

"Not while we are here," the short one replied. "Those old priests are too scared of their own god to ever come down and check."

"We won't be able to get all this stuff tonight without making multiple trips," the tall man said as he picked up his almost-full sack.

"One trip per night is all we get. We will come back tomorrow and get the rest." After he finished, he inspected his own sack. "Who would have imagined that the king would finally decide to pay tribute to that useless god?"

"Watch it," the tall one hissed. "This is still sacred ground *and* his house. We don't want to anger him." His eyes darted all over the room.

"Relax. Obviously he isn't here," the short one said. "This is all ours now, but we have to hurry. Once we leave this horrific place, they will never find us."

With a smile, both men grabbed gold statues and rubies and dumped them into their sacks.

Constantine needed to do something. He couldn't sit there and watch Anubis's temple being dragged out the door. He wasn't sure if he could take two men, but he had to try. Without another thought, Constantine climbed on top of a shelf. The short one was the Alpha, so he needed to take him out first. With no time to turn back, he took a deep breath right before he pounced on the short man.

It was a perfect landing. Constantine's claws were out and when he hit the man, he scratched his way from his face to his belly in one fell swoop. The man screamed, which made his companion drop his bag.

"Shhhh, what are you doing?" the tall man hissed, waving his hands out in front of him.

He pointed to where Constantine sat, licking his paws. "That evil cat attacked me," he said, trying to cover the blood dripping down his face. "Grab him."

The tall man lunged for Constantine, but he was too slow. Constantine had already prepared for it, and he sprang, scratching one of the tall man's leg while he bit his ankle. The man screamed as he bounced up and down on his good leg, which distracted Constantine. He didn't see the short one approaching from behind, and the man squeezed his neck and lifted him in the air. It didn't stop Constantine, though. He just swung around and held on to the man's arm, biting and scratching until more blood flowed like a crimson river of pain.

The man tried to contain his scream, but Constantine went deeper and deeper with his claws. The man swung his arms to try to dislodge the cat, but he wasn't budging. Then, the man did something Constantine didn't see coming. He smacked his arm against the corner of the door.

A loud crack permeated the room, and then Constantine dropped to the ground. Everything hurt as he tried to move, so he laid still, sure the man had broken his back.

"Oh, forgive us, Bastet," the tall man said, covering his heart with his palm. Then he turned to the short man and said, "You killed him."

"Hurry we need to get out of here before anyone finds him," the short man said as he approached the injured cat. He bent over to grab him, but Constantine growled and scratched his hand again.

"Leave him. He still has fight in him. We need to go." The tall man grabbed his sack and ran out the door. The short one tried to grab Constantine one more time, but the cat growled even louder. With a shrug, he slung his bag over his shoulder and followed his friend.

Constantine grimaced as he watched them go. Foam fell from his mouth as he tried to get up. Everything still hurt, but his body wouldn't respond. Constantine laid his head on the ground and closed his eyes. He knew the end was near, and he was going to die alone in this room after he couldn't even help his only friend.

Anubis had watched the two foremen enter the treasure room. It was the same pattern as always: the king sent gold and treasure to the temples and bandits stole it. For a whole day, Anubis had enjoyed the idea of having a real temple like all the other gods, but reality had hit him swift and hard. It was too good to be true, so he came back to reality.

With no reason to stay and watch the thieves take everything, Anubis decided to find Constantine, to bring him food instead. The cat loved food, and Anubis had a feeling he had to fight for it before. Now, he would make sure he never had to fight again.

A scream from the chamber stopped him. There wasn't a soul on this side of the temple besides the foremen. Was there? A horrible, sinking, gut-wrenching feeling shot through Anubis as he walked to the door in time to see Constantine attack the two men.

His heart broke in two. He couldn't interfere. Those were the rules. And when the short man slammed the small feline against the wall, his heart ached. Anubis hadn't even known he had a heart, and he didn't know how he'd come to care for the creature so much in such a little amount of time.

Just like every other creature, when the two foremen passed him, they didn't even know he was in the room.

Anubis watched as Constantine took ragged breaths. It was Anubis's duty to accompany the dead, and even though he would normally wait in the shadows until the soul departed the body, it was different this time. He would keep Constantine company in his last moments and make the journey with him.

He took silent steps toward the cat. When Constantine opened his eyes, he tried to crawl toward Anubis, but his back was broken, and his legs all went in different directions. The sight crushed him, made him want to reach out and heal Constantine, to make it better, but he couldn't. So he did what he could do. He sat next to the cat and Constantine licked Anubis's hand and purred.

Anubis felt something wet running down his face. With his other hand, he reached up and found a tear. He had never cried, not once in his entire life. Also, he barely knew this cat, so why did he care so much?

Without thinking, he picked Constantine up and set him gently on his lap. Damn the consequences. He could heal him, and he would.

"What is it with you and picking fights you can't win?" Anubis's voice cracked from the emotion swimming inside of him.

If he healed him, it would only be temporary. He knew that. Constantine's days were numbered, just like every other creature on this planet. Life was so fragile and so limited. Constantine whined, and Anubis knew it was only a matter of minutes now. He needed to let him go, but as he looked into the big eyes of the fierce little creature below him, he knew he couldn't.

Damn the rules and damn the gods. They had never cared about him anyway. Not a single one of them had ever defended him, either. In fact, not a single one of them had ever even noticed him.

"Constantine, I'm going to make you an offer. I can't force you to take it. It has to be your own free will." Anubis paused.

He'd lost his mind. That was all there was to it. Never had he done something so radical, but he didn't care. It had taken this long to finally find a friend, and he wouldn't allow himself to lose him, even though he was running out of time. They had to move quickly.

"Would you like to be bonded to me? Blink once if yes." Anubis held his breath, knowing that Constantine might prefer to die than be bound to him for eternity. But he didn't because he blinked once. Anubis almost screamed. "You do know this is for all of eternity. Are you sure?" Constantine blinked again and this time bit Anubis on the leg. "Sorry, sorry. Just needed to be sure. Hold still now."

Anubis had never done anything like this before, mainly because he had never wanted to be bonded to anyone. Not once in his entire existence. Why was he doing this for a cat?

Before he got lost in his thoughts again, he lifted Constantine and stared him right in the eyes. Anubis opened his powers, letting them flow until Constantine was covered in glowing light. His powers filled the cat, and he felt the warmth spreading to every part of himself.

"From this day forward, you and I are one, joined together by the power of the gods gifted to me. When it is my time to leave this world, you will join me." Anubis lowered Constantine to his lap. "How do you feel Constantine?"

"Like I was slammed against a wall," Constantine replied.

Anubis laughed. "It worked. I'm amazing," he said.

"I can talk," Constantine said as he examined his paws, then his tail.

"Of course, you can. I couldn't spend eternity trying to decipher every different meow you had," Anubis told Constantine, who was still inspecting himself. "What are you doing?"

"I'm not dead," Constantine said in a soft voice.

"Yes, that's what happens when you bond with a god—at least I think that is what happens." Anubis scratched his head, not exactly sure.

"You don't sound very confident," Constantine said, staring at him.

With a shrug, Anubis confessed, "Well, I haven't exactly done anything like this before."

"Besides human speech, am I different?" Constantine asked, his eyes roaming every inch of his fur.

Anubis leaned in and nodded. "There is one big difference. You are Immortal now."

"Really?" Constantine asked, extending his claws in one paw and slamming it into Anubis's thigh.

"Ouch." Anubis rubbed his legs. "You are definitely a lot stronger, and less fragile, which is good since you love starting fights. The rest we will figure it out in time, I guess." He gave Constantine a glance. He really had no clue how his powers would affect the cat. He didn't really care either. Constantine was alive, which was what mattered.

"Fight, right. Those men will come back to steal the rest of your stuff. You need to stop them," Constantine said in a rush.

"Constantine, I told you, I can't get involved," Anubis admitted in a soft voice, his eyes looking at the ground. "I'm sure I already crossed a line by giving you my powers." His eyes looked out the window, and he looked anywhere besides at Constantine.

"Can I get involved?" Constantine asked, stretching his back. "Now that I'm totally healed and all."

"Of course, you are. You will heal much faster from now on," Anubis replied.

Constantine stretched again, moving his body in so many strange ways. "So, can I get involved, then?" Constantine repeated his question.

"Considering they almost killed you, I say you are involved. Why do you ask?" Anubis frowned.

"Perfect. As your representative, I got some people to visit," Constantine told Anubis, flashing an evil grin that showed all his canines.

"My what?" Anubis asked, looking around. "What just happened?"

"Simple. As my master, I have to defend your properties," Constantine said slowly.

"Constantine, I'm not your master. You are your own master. We are partners. How about that?" Anubis asked.

"That is so much better. I hated the idea of having to bow down," Constantine said, licking the inside of his leg.

Anubis laughed again. The cat had a sense of humor. Who knew? "I have created a monster."

"I have work to do," Constantine told Anubis right before he stepped out of the room.

"I have a feeling the world is not ready for Constantine." Anubis shook his head. "What am I saying? *I'm* not ready for Constantine." Anubis watched his crazy cat leave the chamber. "Too late now."

Chapter Four

Constantine had a simple, although brilliant, plan. He would wake up the high priest, convince him of the crime the foremen committed, and then have them arrested. It wouldn't take any time at all. After all, he was a talking cat with powers from Anubis. After he got this out of the way, then he could go back to figuring out what being Immortal meant.

The priests were the only ones allowed to stay in Saqqara permanently. The workers were given temporary housing in small tents outside. The priests had rooms on the opposite side of the treasure room. The Temple was a big square, and the only doors were near the priests' rooms. For some reason, they believed that was all the security they needed.

Constantine made his way around the temple to the high priest's room. He heard once that the high priest was a real light sleeper. Maybe that was the reason the robbers had taken the chambers of the apprentices.

Constantine snuck in the room. Compared to the barrenness of the temple, the high priest's room was extravagant. He had fur rugs on the floor, fancy sheets on his bed, and a canopy. The room had a weird smell to it, though, and as Constantine examined the room, he found the source. The weird priest had incense burning under his bed. Constantine could only stare at it, confused as to why.

It took him a minute to pull himself away from the strange bowl, and once he did, he jumped on the small table by the bed. He glared at the priest, making sure his look was convincing, but also calm. The last thing he wanted to do was startle anyone.

"Priest. Listen to my voice and wake up," Constantine said, trying to make his voice sound deeper.

"Ah…ah…" the priest muttered.

"What? I said get up and listen to me," Constantine demanded.

"Come back later," the priest mumbled.

"Wake up, you old fool. I was sent by Anubis!" Constantine shouted at the priest.

The priest didn't wake up. Instead he rolled so he was no longer facing Constantine, which infuriated him, but what could he do? He left the room, kicking every rock and pebble on his way out. He needed a more direct approach because subtlety didn't work with these people.

Constantine made his way to the priests's apprentice's room, which was opposite of the main entrance. The temple was constructed to ensure people wouldn't wander through the place without being seen. A foolish plan in Constantine's eyes.

Constantine entered the room. He didn't hesitate as he climbed on the bed and jumped on the man's chest, plopping down and making himself comfortable.

"Wake up and look into my eyes," Constantine told the apprentice, but nothing happened. Constantine did not have time to waste. He backed up and then slapped him across the face with his paw. At least he had retracted his claws.

"Ah, what's going on?" the apprentice mumbled.

"Listen here, boy. I work for Anubis and need you to wake up." Constantine had his eyes about six inches from the man's eyeball, and he glared at him.

"Ahhhhh," the apprentice screamed as he shoved at Constantine. "I'm possessed." The apprentice hopped from his bed and ran out the door.

"Well, that didn't go according to my plan," Constantine muttered as he jumped from the bed and headed toward the other chambers.

Anubis was reclining on a soft couch when Constantine walked into the soon-to-be workshop area. Anubis was popping grapes into his mouth while some strange contraption played music. Constantine had no idea what those things were and how they could move by themselves. He also didn't have the time to worry about it.

Constantine marched right over to Anubis and jumped on the strange couch. "What are you doing?"

"Eating these little round things. I think they are called grapes," Anubis replied as he popped another grape in his mouth.

"Why? I thought you didn't need to eat." Constantine examined the bowl of grapes, then stabbed one with a claw and dropped it in his mouth.

"I don't. I'm just practicing for when my people come over to worship me," Anubis said as Constantine spit his grape to the floor. "I saw this on one of my trips. A king had people feeding him these things while others fanned him with giant leaves."

"You should tell them to feed you something else because these little balls are sour," Constantine said to Anubis as he pushed grapes around in the bowl.

"Maybe they are not ripe yet," Anubis told him.

"How do you know when they are ripe?" Constantine asked, not sure why the bowl had different colored grapes.

"No clue. We might need to get a human for this," Anubis said, dropping the grape back in the bowl and jumping off the couch.

"By the way, I think something happened to my vision. I got all these other colors popping up that I never had before, and everything is so bright," Constantine told Anubis, rubbing his eyes.

"Interesting, it seems I gave you my sight. I wonder if you are going to get my hearing as well," Anubis said, more to himself than Constantine.

"Great. I will let you know if that happens," Constantine said in a dry tone.

"What happened? When you left, you were happy, ready to conquer the world. Probably the temple to be more exact," Anubis said, examining the basket of fabrics against the wall.

"Have you ever considered being the god of something else, like food or drinks?" Constantine asked as he dropped his head on his paws. "Everyone is terrified of you. It doesn't help that you have the head of a giant dog."

"It is a jackal," Anubis corrected him, pointing to his face.

"That is even worse. You have the head of the animals that eat the flesh of the dead." Constantine covered his eyes with his paws.

"This is not my fault. Everything else was taken. I got stuck as the God of Death." Anubis frowned. "Trust me, nobody wants to be be friends with the God of Death."

"Tell me about it," Constantine said. "I spoke with every priest and those annoying apprentices. The ones who were awake ran out in panic, convinced I was the guardian of the underworld, there to take them away." Constantine rolled over and let his arm fall off the couch.

"That's not bad. We could use that," Anubis said, rubbing his hands together.

"We want them to lock those two foremen up, not rush the gates of the underworld," Constantine said, almost hissing.

"Don't get mad at me. I told you already that everyone avoids me," Anubis said in a childlike voice.

"Adults are so stuck in their ways," Constantine said, then he jumped straight up, landing on his feet. "That's it. I need to get to the city."

"What?" Anubis asked, staring at Constantine. He held a small figurine in his hand, and when Constantine opened his mouth to talk, he chucked it towards the wall

"Hey, those things are expensive," Constantine told Anubis as he watched Anubis toss it aside.

"It's worthless. This stupid, little thing will not help you at all in the afterlife. Not to mention it's hideous." Anubis looked at it one more time and shook himself. "But don't change the subject. Why do you need to head to the city?"

"We need children," Constantine told him.

"On purpose?" Anubis asked as he tossed more figurines around.

"Yes. Children love helping others, which means they will help us," Constantine told him.

"I like your plan, but how are you going to get to the city? The thieves took off with the chariot," Anubis said.

"You can take me," Constantine quickly replied.

"That is considered me getting involved," Anubis told him.

"Fine. I'll find a way," Constantine finished and jumped off the couch. "And stop throwing that stuff around. You are not going to have anything nice to put in your worship temple."

"A lot of the stuff here is useless. Those two thieves took most of the good stuff." Anubis pouted.

"Fine, we will get your stuff back. Right now, though, I need to get us people." Constantine walked out of the room, leaving Anubis to play with the weird toys.

Constantine had no way of getting back to the city before dawn. He needed to get help to stop the thieves. He meandered to the edge of Saqqara and peered down the delta of the Nile. It was beautiful. The stars reflected on the river and the palm trees slowly swayed with the breeze. With Anubis's powers in him, the world looked brighter, sharper. Even his sense of smell was more refined. That's when he noticed them: the terrors of the night. It was a pack of jackals, and they were prowling towards him.

If only I was as big and fast as one of them. Constantine thought to himself. With just that thought, his body changed. His paws grew, his face elongated, and his body became fluid and bigger.

"Oh no. Anubis!" Constantine screamed.

"Constantine, where are you?" Anubis said from behind him.

Constantine gasped. "How did you get here?"

"I heard you calling me in my mind. But Constantine, is that you?" Anubis asked him as he slowly approached.

"I think so. What is happening to me?" Constantine asked, looking at his paws, his body, and the way the whole world looked from this new, higher angle.

"Your body shifted to a jackal. What were you doing?" Anubis asked, kneeling next to Constantine as he examined his new form.

"I heard the pack coming and wished I was one of them. Am I stuck like this forever?" Constantine's breaths came heavier and drool dribbled from his mouth. Panic had taken root, and he had a feeling it wasn't going anywhere anytime soon.

"I doubt it. I can shift to whatever form I like. Think of being you and let's see what happens." Anubis took a few steps back, giving Constantine room.

Constantine blew out a couple breaths, then closed his eyes. He imagined his small, slick frame, his bright stripes, and his delicate features. *Bring back the handsome me.*

The thought initiated a shift and before he opened his eyes, he felt his body shrinking. When he opened his eyes again, he found his own paws.

"Yes! I'm back!" Constantine screamed as he rolled around the dirt in celebration.

"If you keep that up, it's going to take you forever to get all your fur clean again," Anubis told him as he pointed at the mud covering him.

Constantine looked down and jumped straight up. "Oh, you are so right." He gave himself a little shake, trying to clean his fur off.

"Can you shift to a human?" Anubis asked after Constantine finished licking the dirt off him.

"Why would I ever want to do that?" Constantine asked, giving Anubis an evil glare.

"Just try," Anubis told him.

"Fine," Constantine said, rolling his eyes.

He took a deep breath and imagined one of the priests from the temple. The way humans moved and walked. *Make me a human*, Constantine told himself, but nothing happened. His body never shifted.

"Thank you, thank you. I'm still me," Constantine said, kissing his paws and rubbing himself.

"You are so dramatic," Anubis told him with a smirk. "It seems you are only able to shift to four-legged, furry animals. Not bad at all. You can also communicate with me if you focus." Anubis sat on the ground and stared at Constantine like he was the most interesting thing in the world.

"Why are you looking at me like that?" Constantine asked, backing away from Anubis.

"Constantine, can you hear me?" Anubis asked, but his lips never moved.

"Ahhh! How did you do that?" Constantine asked, his eyes darting every which way, like he'd turned into a feral, wild cat. He walked in circles, rubbing his ears furiously.

"Stop that or you're going to make yourself sick," Anubis told him, and Constantine slowed down. "You try it this time. Think of me, start with my name, and then say something. Can you do that?" The words came out slow, steady.

Constantine just nodded.

He couldn't focus while facing Anubis, so he turned around to face the Nile. He closed his eyes and cleared his mind of all the confusing thoughts floating through it.

He pictured Anubis's face in his mind and when the image was clear, he spoke. "Anubis, this is scary." That was all he could think to say.

"Yes, it is, but it will get easier," Anubis replied.

Constantine's fur stood on end. "You heard me?" He faced Anubis. "Can you read my mind?"

"Of course not." Anubis folded his arms over his chest and shook his head. "We can communicate across distances, but definitely no mind reading. Besides, I would be afraid to know what goes on inside your head." Anubis poked Constantine in the side. "It does make me feel better, though. At least I know you can call for help when you get in trouble."

"What makes you think I'll get in trouble?" Constantine asked, batting his big eyes at Anubis. Although he had a feeling he didn't play innocent as well as he thought he did.

"It's you, Constantine. Trouble finds you in your sleep." Anubis angled his head as he stared at the cat., who was now examining the horizon.

"You might have a point." Constantine paused, his gaze roaming the horizon. "How fast do you think those jackals run?" He pointed towards the pack not too far from them now.

"They are pretty fast and very deadly. Are you planning to outrun them?" Anubis asked.

"Not at all. I was hoping to join them," Constantine said with a wicked grin. He started trotting in the direction of the jackals. Anubis followed a little further behind.

Constantine reached the pack and they looked vicious. They growled and spit as they circled the two of them.

"Who is the Alpha here?" Constantine asked in the jackals' language.

"Who wants to know?" a tall and sleek jackal replied in what sounded like a female voice.

"The name is Constantine. I need a guide back to the city," Constantine said, holding eye contact with the female.

"You would never make it in your shape, little one." The female's mocking laughter drifted through the air, and soon, the rest of the pack joined in.

Constantine stared at the powerful muscles of her body, the angle of her face, and the shape of her paws. *I want to be a jackal*, Constantine told himself and his body immediately complied. The shift was faster this time. He was a few inches taller than the female and his black fur was shining in the night.

"How?" The female growled, baring her teeth.

"Calm down, now," Constantine told her. "I'm not looking for dominance, just a guide. Can you do that?" he asked, bowing his head. A tingle shot down his spine when the rest of the pack bowed to him.

"It will be our honor, Constantine," the female replied with a soft purr.

"I'm so in trouble!" Anubis shouted from behind Constantine.

"What? Are you okay?" Constantine asked as he turned to Anubis, searching for anything that might be wrong.

"I gave you dominion over animals." Anubis paced around the group, his arms flying everywhere. "The gods are going to bury me alive for centuries. They are going to make me the god of sheep, or maybe I will get lucky and they will give me camels. How am I ever going to explain this?"

Constantine strolled over to him and pushed him.

"Ouch. What was that for?" Anubis asked as he almost tripped on a rock.

"Now who is being dramatic? Get a hold of yourself. You are making us look bad." He angled his head towards the pack.

"Oh, sorry about that," Anubis said, waving his hand at the group.

"I don't think they can understand you," Constantine said to Anubis. "Don't mind my friend; he had a long night," Constantine said to the jackals.

"I already know too many languages, so I'm not interested in learning the animal ones." Anubis rubbed his head, which he did only when he was upset or nervous.

"Not a problem, I'll handle the conversations with the animal kingdom," Constantine said, licking his side to make the fur shine even more.

"What am I going to do?" Anubis asked, a panicked look in his eyes.

"Don't tell them," Constantine said with a huge smile.

"What? How?" Anubis asked as he stopped moving, so still he almost looked like a statue.

"Do you honestly think all the gods share everything with you?" Constantine asked. "They don't even invite you to their parties. Why do you even care what they think, or say for that matter?" He gave him a hard look as he waited for his response.

"You are right. None of them ever come to see me. Why do I need to give them any power over me, over my thoughts? My actions?" Anubis said in a calmer voice. "I think you are a bad influence, Constantine."

"I've heard that before." Constantine grinned again. "Now that we settled that, I need to head to the city. Found me some guides." He flicked his head towards the pack.

"Good luck, but please don't burn down any temples," Anubis said, and Constantine gave him the big, soft, innocent-eyed look.

"I'm serious. I don't need that annoying Ptah coming around to complain about his city." He rubbed his head again.

"He would never connect anything back to you," Constantine replied in a confident tone.

"You smell like me. Trust me, there won't be any doubt I was involved," Anubis said with his arms crossed. "Promise me."

"Fine. I won't burn any temples," Constantine finally agreed, if only to calm Anubis down. "Time to go." He headed towards the pack. He needed to get away before Anubis thought of any more rules for him.

Constantine reached the pack and signaled to the Alpha. Without a sound, the pack took off. Constantine had never moved this fast in his life. He felt alive as he easily kept up with the jackals' speed and agility. The earth flew beneath his paws, and he smiled as he realized he could run like that all night long.

Chapter Five

The jackals took Constantine to the edge of Inbu-Hedj. When they arrived, Constantine's breaths came heavy, but considering how much territory they had crossed, they weren't heavy enough. He looked at the white walls of the palace, and even at night, they glowed with pride.

"This is as far as we go, Constantine," the female Alpha told him.

"This is perfect. Thank you. I wouldn't want you guys to get hurt on my account," Constantine replied with as much kindness in his voice as possible.

"Will you need a guide back?" the female asked.

"I'm hoping to bring a few friends back with me, so probably not. But thank you for the offer." Constantine bowed his head to her.

"We will scout the desert in case you need us. See you soon, Constantine." The female bowed to him this time, then led her pack back towards the desert, disappearing in a blur of speed.

Constantine looked at the sky, judging the time. Dawn would be coming soon. He needed to cross the marketplace and make it to the other side of the city to Ammon's house. Time was of the essence and he didn't have enough to waste hiding in the shadows. With a silent chuckle, Constantine thought of his promise to Anubis. He couldn't burn anything down, but he had never promised not to have a few fights. He smiled. It was going to be a long night.

Inbu-Hedj was deserted at night, but Constantine knew the guards were out patrolling the city. As he entered, it dawned on him that he remained in jackal form, so he willed his body to shift. When it did, surprise clawed at him. He had actually liked that form.

After a few minutes of adjusting to his normal body, Constantine took off towards Ammon's house. This time in the city, he didn't care who saw him. He was on a mission from the god Anubis to be more precise.

It was amazing how quickly he could move when he wasn't afraid. Constantine had crossed the city and made it to the market place in record time. He wondered if Anubis's powers were also giving him speed. After a quick reflection, he realized they must, but they did more than that. They also took his appetite away. He didn't crave food or water—a fact he despised. He loved food, at least he had when he could get his hands on it.

"Well, well. Look what the Nile dragged back in." Constantine stiffened. He heard the voices, but he didn't see the group, although he knew who would be in it.

From behind a large statue of Menes, the leader of the disciplinarians walked out. Constantine had heard rumors about him. He was strong, powerful, and had jaws that could break a cat's throat. Behind the chief, his three adversaries from the previous night were walking up. They did not look nearly as bad as Constantine had hoped. From the other side, even more cats moved his way, leaving him surrounded.

"I don't have time to play with you guys today. Move out of my way," Constantine told them as his ears stood straight up. He was hesitant. He had no idea if he could take them all, even with his new powers.

"Oh, just look at him. He thinks he is so brave. You are going to be dead trash when we are done with you." The chief prowled towards him.

The chief was trying to intimidate him, and he thought it was working. He'd brought his sharp claws out, bared his teeth, and made his fur stand on end. Constantine gave him a bored look. He wasn't afraid, not in the least. In fact, he wasn't even impressed.

A wicked smiled played at his lips when it hit him. Anubis's powers hadn't made him brave, they had just amplified his own courage. He was a force to be reckoned with, and he always had been.

"Nice speech, but I really don't have time for you. Can we do this on the next full moon?" Constantine asked calmly.

The chief laughed at Constantine right before he charged. Laughter erupted from the crowd, and Constantine watched every detail unfold around him, almost as if in slow motion. He didn't run. Fear hadn't touched him, and he knew it wouldn't.

When the chief reached him, his teeth aimed right for Constantine's neck and a growl echoing through the plaza, Constantine did a smooth side shuffle and dodged the powerful jaws. Before the chief could recover from his miss, Constantine attacked, sending him flying across the market with only a slap.

The crowd froze. The whole market went silent. Even Constantine did, because in truth, he hadn't expected his punches to be so strong or his reflexes to be so quick. He felt great. Reckoning day had come and he was ready to take on the world.

For another moment, he watched the chief still lying on the cold floor, knocked out. He reveled in that moment, and then he faced the rest of his enemies.

"The name is Constantine, and I recommend you remember it," Constantine told the crowd in a voice colder than death. "Leave." The command in his voice left no room for argument. The cats scattered every which way, and in less than three blinks, the market was deserted.

"I could get used to this," Constantine told himself. He glanced back at the sky and watched dawn coming from the east. "Oh no, running out of time."

Constantine took off at a full sprint.

The working part of the city was already bursting with life by the time Constantine reached it. Unlike the temples and wealthy areas, the lower class had to work harder to survive. Ammon was at the door of his house when Constantine came rushing down the road.

Unfortunately, Constantine had failed to judge his actual speed. With no time to stop, he collided with Ammon. Both of them tumbled to the ground, and Constantine landed on top of Ammon when they finally stopped spinning.

"Oh, wow, that hurt," Ammon mumbled, sitting up and dusting off his shirt.

"Ammon, listen. I need your help," Constantine told him as he stared at the poor boy only inches from his face.

"Ahhhh!" screamed Ammon. "You can talk. That's impossible," he said, pushing Constantine off him and getting as far away as he could while still on the ground.

"Shhh. Do you want everyone to hear you?" Constantine asked him.

Ammon stiffened. "You can talk," he whispered. "By the gods, how?" His eyes drifted to the road.

"You can thank Anubis for that," Constantine said with a smirk. "Should we go inside to have this conversation?"

"Yes, yes, of course," Ammon said, quickly bouncing off the ground and rushing back inside his house. Constantine followed at a more dignified pace.

Inside the house, everything was still dark. The house was small but clean and tidy. Constantine knew that the front room served as the dining area, kitchen, and family room. In the back, Ammon shared one room with his mother and sister.

Constantine had always admired Ammon's love for his family.

Ammon lit a candle on the table. "You serve Anubis now?" His words were quiet, and Constantine almost immediately realized why. His family still slept.

Constantine jumped next to the candle and sat. "I'm technically his partner," he replied. "It's a long story, but the bottom line is we both need your help."

Ammon frowned. "Me, why?" Ammon asked, backing away from the table. "He is a god."

"Yes, I know all that, but he has some weird rules. Something about not interfering directly with the affairs of men." Constantine rolled his eyes again. "But thieves were at his new temple disguised as foremen and they are coming back."

"Shouldn't you be telling the priests this?" Ammon said as he slowly moved away from Constantine.

"I tried, but it's hard to talk to adults. That's why I'm here." Constantine walked to the edge of the table.

"How could I possibly help you?" Ammon asked. "Look cat, it's one thing to take in one of your friends, but my family needs me. I can't miss work," Ammon told Constantine as he moved towards the door.

"The name is Constantine," he told him, which made Ammon stop moving. "Ammon, I'm offering a chance to help a god and have a better life for you and your family. Don't you want that?" Constantine asked, pointing towards the back room.

"I have to go. You can stay here if you like, just don't wake my sister." Before Constantine could say anything else, Ammon was out the door.

"Well, that didn't go as I planned," Constantine said out loud as he made himself comfortable on the table.

"He is scared," a soft, little voice said from behind him.

Constantine spun around, ready to attack. "Hey, it's you," he said, recognizing the little kitten he had saved.

"Hi. Ammon named me Moses." The little kitten smiled.

"Hi Moses. I have a name as well," Constantine told the kitten.

"I heard. Constantine. I like it." Moses got closer and sat next to Constantine. "You can speak to humans now."

"I can do all sorts of things now, but it's a long story," Constantine said, staring out the door.

"Ammon wants to help everyone, but his sister is sick and there is not enough food for the rest of the day," Moses explained to Constantine. "The foremen in the fields are cutting their wages and things are getting harder. He has too much pressure for a little boy."

Moses was really bright for one so young.

"That *is* a lot of pressure for a little boy," Constantine agreed.

"You work for Anubis, right? Does that mean you could you help them?" Moses asked, bouncing on the table. "If they see you can help them, then maybe they will help you back."

Constantine was thinking the same thing. Anubis didn't have any followers, probably because nobody thought he could do anything for them. It was time Constantine changed that. He just needed to convince Anubis.

"Let me see what I can do. Keep an eye on them Moses," Constantine told the little kitten as he walked out of the house.

Chapter Six

I t took Constantine a full day to convince Anubis to help him. The last thing he wanted to do was heal the living, but Constantine didn't let up and finally wore him down. Anubis agreed to meet him at the house with healing herbs and food.

Constantine waited as patiently as he could, kicking rocks around the road. Anubis appeared in front of the little mud house in full human form. He had jet-black hair with a defined jaw line, olive skin, and deep blue eyes.

"What took you so long?" Constantine asked Anubis as soon as he laid eyes on him.

"It takes some time to figure out what healing herbs to bring to a house when you are the god of death." Anubis's tone dripped with sarcasm. "You do know we have other gods for these things, like Taweret?"

"You are too obsessed with this god of death thing. We need to work on your identity," Constantine told Anubis, looking up at him. "Who is this Taweret again?"

"The hippo goddess, protector of women and children," Anubis replied.

"Have you guys considered combining all this protection stuff into just one god? It gets kind of confusing remembering which god to pray to for what." Constantine's gaze trailed up and down Anubis. "What happened to your eyes?"

"What is wrong with my eyes?" Anubis asked as he touched both of them.

"I'm not sure. Get down here so I can see you better." Constantine stood on his back leg and stretched while Anubis bent down. "They are blue. Why are your eyes blue?"

"There is nothing wrong with my eyes," Anubis said, standing up straight and avoiding Constantine. "Blue is my natural color. This is what my human form looks like." He pointed at himself.

"You are going to stick out here," Constantine responded, gesturing to the neighborhood.

"I'm not changing them. It is not like I am getting a house here." Anubis stuck out his tongue, making Constantine shake his head. "Let's do this before I change my mind." He grabbed the two sacks that were lying next to him. Constantine hadn't seen them until now. He guessed he hadn't been paying enough attention.

"We need to wait. Ammon won't be home till sunset," Constantine told Anubis,

"So, all your rushing was for nothing, then, since now we are stuck waiting. This is crazy. I'm going back to napping. Give me a call me when you are ready."

Constantine opened his mouth to reply, but Anubis had already disappeared.

"Temperamental god," Constantine muttered.

After finding a nice spot by an alley, Constantine got comfortable. His senses were on full alert and he wondered why no other cats were around. Well, no other cats besides Moses. Focusing, he took in the area and didn't see a soul, not human or animal.

"That is so strange," Constantine mumbled.

"What is strange?" Moses asked from behind.

"It took you long enough to come out," Constantine told Moses.

"I tried, but he is scary," Moses confessed.

"Who is scary?" Constantine asked, but he had a feeling he already knew the answer.

"That was Anubis, right? Even in human form, he smells different," Moses admitted. "There is something about him that pushes everyone away. Can't you feel it?" The kitten stared hard at Constantine.

"I'm bonded to him, so I doubt I would notice it. But even before I was, it never bothered me," Constantine said.

"You are a brave soul," Moses told him.

"I recommend you find your courage, though. He is coming back," Constantine said to Moses.

Moses swallowed hard. "I'll try."

"I know you will," Constantine said as he patted the kitten's shoulder.

Sunset came quicker than Constantine expected. He let his eyes drift closed while listening to Moses telling stories of everything that had happened while he was gone. Moses even filled him in on the rumors of the magical cat that beat up the chief, and Constantine couldn't help but smile.

Magical is an understatement, he thought with a snicker.

Before he could fall completely asleep, Ammon and one of his friends came home.

"Who is that?" Constantine whispered.

"Pilis, Ammon's best friend," Moses said. "His parents died when he was born, so he spends most of his days here with Ammon."

"Anubis, it's time!" Constantine shouted through his mind.

"No need to shout. I can hear you just fine, even when you use your normal voice," Anubis replied, standing over both cats.

Moses screamed, and he didn't stop for at least a minute.

"Do you have to sneak up on people?" Constantine asked with a hand over his heart. Now if only he could catch his breath.

"Why are you surprised? You are the one who called me," Anubis said, crossing his arms over his chest.

"I don't know. I guess I expected a reply before you appeared," Constantine admitted.

"That takes too long. Let's go. I was in the middle of inspecting my offerings at the temple," Anubis told the cats as he stepped towards the house.

"Offerings? What offerings?" Constantine ran to catch up with Anubis.

"It seems your little visit to the priests prompted them to believe I was being neglected. Now we have tons of offerings and the temple is almost done." When he uttered the last word, Anubis almost danced from the joy shining from him.

"Not what I was hoping for, but okay," Constantine said in a low tone.

A crowd of workers covered the streets, but they quickly cleared out, most likely ducking into their homes. When the two cats and Anubis arrived at the door, it was Anubis who knocked. Then he waited, tapping his foot against the ground.

Pilis answered the door, but Constantine could see Ammon peeking out from behind him.

"Can we help you?" Pilis asked.

"No. Actually, I am here to help you," Anubis told the boys.

"He is with me," Constantine said, squeezing between Anubis's legs.

"By the gods, you were right. He does talk." Pilis looked like he was trying to melt into the door.

"Can we come in? My friend is here to help your sister," Constantine asked as he watched Moses sneak back into the house.

"I don't know." Ammon inspected Anubis carefully.

"Ammon, who is at the door?" a female voice asked. A fragile-looking, older lady appeared in the doorway.

"Mother, this is…" Ammon trailed off, unable to finish his sentence.

"I'm Constantine," he jumped in. "And this is my healer friend. Can we come in?" he asked the mother, keeping his voice calm.

"By the mercy of Bastet, the rumors are true." The mother dropped to her knees and bowed before Constantine. "If the goddess wishes you to bless us with your presence, it is an honor."

"I technically work for—"

Anubis shoved Constantine, stopping his words. Then he cut in and said, "What Constantine means is we are grateful." Anubis's tone sounded like silk running down your spine.

The boys and the mother moved and Constantine and Anubis entered the house. The mother wouldn't meet Anubis's eyes as he examined her.

"Where is your daughter?" Anubis asked.

"In the back. I'll take you." Her words rushed out of her, nervous energy spiking each one.

"No need." Anubis placed one of the large sacks on the small table. "If you don't mind preparing a meal instead, that would be very helpful. You should find plenty of food in there." Anubis headed towards the back and Constantine followed right behind him.

"We need to work on your conversational skills with humans," Constantine whispered to Anubis.

"How often am I going to have conversations with the dead?" Anubis replied in a soft hiss. "Let's get this done before there are any more rumors spread about you or me."

"It is not my fault people love me," Constantine said, wiping his face.

Anubis turned away with an eye roll, then he sat next to the girl on the tiny bed. This room was a lot smaller than the one in the front, and the only furniture were two beds, both about the same size. A small candle lit the corner of the room, but gave very little light anywhere else.

Constantine searched through the second sack Anubis had carried in. "Which one of these weird trees do you need?" Constantine asked as he buried his head inside the sack.

"I have no idea," Anubis replied.

"What? Then why are you carrying this?" Constantine asked as he popped his head out of the sack.

"I'm a god. I don't need herbs to heal. I just thought it would look really suspicious if I showed up empty handed," Anubis told him as he pointed towards the other room with his head.

"Good point. Now what?" Constantine asked, joining Anubis on the bed.

"I guess we pretend to mix this stuff? To make it look real?" Anubis shrugged as he leaned over the herbs, then his lip curled up in disgust. "This stuff smells awful." He plugged his nose as he picked up the first bottle.

Constantine grinned as Anubis mixed herbs into the bottle, pretending to make an ointment. After the plants, he added some other things to the jar. Constantine didn't know what they were, but he did agree that the herbs smelled worse than the dead.

"I hope that stuff doesn't kill her," Constantine whispered.

"It won't kill her, but it might make *us* sick." Anubis covered his nose with his hand. "Are you ready?"

"What's next?" Constantine asked as he slowly backed away from the horrible smell.

"We put this stuff on her," Anubis told him.

"Do we have to? Can we just put it next to her and tell everyone that the fumes will cure her?" Constantine asked, staying as far away as he could.

"I like that. Watch the door." Anubis put his hands over the girl's head and heart while Constantine kept watch.

The process didn't take very long. Constantine only had enough time to glance at the three people in the other room as they cooked, and when he turned back, Anubis was done and the young girl was sitting up in the bed, her breathing normal again.

"How do you feel?" Anubis asked the little girl.

"Better. Who are you?" she asked. "Does your cat really talk or was I dreaming?"

Anubis and Constantine exchanged a quick glance. "He is technically not *mine* but his own being. And yes, he does talk," Anubis finally answered.

"Can I pet him?" The little girl leaned towards Constantine.

"There is no touching this fabulous fur unless you want to lose an arm," Constantine answered, baring his teeth.

The girl jerked her hands away from him. "Where is my mother?" Her voice sounded loud in the small room. "Mother?" Panic set her tone this time as she screamed.

The mother rushed in the room holding a ladle. When she saw her little girl sitting up, she dropped the ladle and hurried to the bed, falling to her knees in front of her baby as she wrapped her arms around her. Tears of joy ran down her face.

"No need for tears. She is going to be okay," Anubis told her, touching her back. The mother's shoulders dropped and she breathed so much easier with that touch.

"Anubis, what did you do to her?" Constantine asked through his mind, proud of himself that he didn't freak out. The mind talks were getting easier every time he did them.

"I healed the illness in her chest. She had whatever her daughter had," Anubis replied through his mind, but he winked at Constantine.

"It's time for me to be going," Anubis told the mother as he grabbed his sack of herbs.

"How can we repay you?" the mother asked, tears streaming down her cheeks.

"Friends of Constantine's are friends of mine, so there is no need for payment."

Before the mother could reply, Anubis left the room, so she turned to Constantine and said, "Thank you."

"Anytime," Constantine said right before he chased after Anubis, but he had already disappeared.

"How can he move that fast?" Constantine asked, not to anyone in particular.

"I'm sure when you are a god, you can do anything," Ammon answered from the far side of the room.

"How did you know?" Constantine asked as he jumped on the table.

"Constantine, he looked too young to be a healer. On top of that, there was a strange air around him," Ammon answered. "What do you want from us?" He crossed his arms and stared at Constantine.

"Relax. We don't want your souls or anything," Constantine shot out.

"He saved my sister. I probably owe him that and more," Ammon answered as he walked to the table.

"Why are humans so dramatic?" Constantine asked in reply. "Listen, Anubis doesn't have any real followers. The priests he has are old, broken, and some just useless. We need to find the robbers who broke into his temple yesterday and retrieve what they stole before they return for more."

"That sounds simple," Pilis said.

"The problem is, they are the foremen for the artisans at Saqqara," Constantine added, not meeting their eyes.

"Oh, that is a problem." Pilis turned a strange shade of green.

"Foremen rule every crew. If we try to go to the guards without evidence, we will be thrown in jail," Ammon told Constantine.

"That's why we need your help," Constantine said in a soft voice.

"We will help," Ammon's mother answered from the bedroom door.

"Mother!" Ammon shouted.

"No son, we will help." His mother's tone left no room for argument. "Anubis cured Nane and me," she added, and the words were barely audible.

"Mother, why didn't you tell me?" Ammon rushed at his mother.

"To worry you more?" She shook her head. "Never." The mother touched her son's cheek and smiled at him. "If the god Anubis blessed our home, then we will be his devoted servants forever."

"Can we just start with the robbers first and worry about the whole eternity thing later?" Constantine said, unsure what gods did with devoted servants. He'd have to ask Anubis.

"Sounds like we need to find where they are hiding the treasures and what their plans are," the mother told the group. "Ammon and Pilis, gather all your friends. We need to find that location tonight."

"Yes, mother," Ammon said, then he ran out the door.

"Yes, Nefret," Pilis replied, already following Ammon.

"Thank you," Constantine told the mother.

"Thank you, Constantine. You have brought life into this house," the mother replied.

"It's going to be a long night of waiting," Constantine told the mother. "Make sure to feed your daughter and yourself. Also, try to rest. You will need it after the healing Anubis performed."

"We will," she said as she moved towards the kitchen to get food. She placed a bowl filled to the top on the floor in front of

Constantine, and another in front of Moses, then smiled once more before heading back to the room carrying two more bowls.

Constantine was restless and started pacing a circle around the small table. He couldn't just wait around doing nothing. He decided to scout the city as well, hoping to find information. Without saying goodbye, Constantine walked out of the house on his own mission.

Chapter Seven

C onstantine roamed the city, hoping to find anyone willing to talk to him. He stopped when he discovered he stood in front of the great Ptah temple in the middle of the city. If Anubis found out he had visited that temple, he would kill Constantine. Just as he turned around, eyes glowed from inside the temple, looking right in his direction. Normally, the temple's enforcer cats would've challenged him by now, but nobody had appeared.

Except the glowing eyes.

Curiosity pulled him inside. The temple was beautiful, nothing like the small, simple chamber that was being created for Anubis. All the greatest artisans had paid their respect to Ptah with their work. Constantine was impressed and annoyed. It wasn't fair this weird guy had so many followers when he never took care of his people. Meanwhile, Anubis never missed a burial. He always showed up at every ceremony to guide the souls to their afterlife.

From the far end of the temple, Constantine heard footsteps. He picked up his pace as he followed the sound. His steps were silent on the stone floor—probably another perk of Anubis's powers swirling inside of him.

When the sound of footsteps stopped, Constantine kept going and pounced, with no idea what to expect. Luckily, he only landed on two temple cats. He couldn't have been more thankful that it hadn't been humans.

"Oh mighty and great Constantine, please don't kill us," one of the cats begged.

"Please. Spare us," the other said.

Constantine held one by the neck and the other by the tail, and their words made a smile stretch over his lips. "'Mighty and great.' I like that," Constantine told the cats. "But why do you think I'm here to kill you?" he asked the cats without letting go.

"Rumor has it that you have returned to take revenge on all who have humiliated you." The words rushed out of the cat being held by the tail.

"We are sorry. We didn't know Anubis was your protector," the other said, struggling to talk with Constantine's paw on his neck.

"You mean to tell me all it would've taken was me telling you a god was on my side to make you stay away?" Constantine asked with a mocking laugh. "What do you take me for?" He hissed and showed his teeth.

"No, please don't kill us," the two cats whined in unison.

"Not so brave without your enforcers around," Constantine told them sweetly. "Guess what? I'm feeling generous today. I will spare your life for information."

"Anything you want, Master Constantine," they replied.

Constantine released the cats slowly, and they bowed before him. He shook his head. "I need to find the two foremen that came back from Saqqara with a giant bounty. Find them tonight and report back to me at Ammon's house, and then you will be spared," he growled.

"Yes, Master." Both cats shook with fear, but soon they had stood and trounced out of the temple's entrance.

I could get used to this, Constantine told himself.

Now that all his dirty work was being done by the best spies in the kingdom, he had no idea what to do. As he looked around the temple, he decided to see what Anubis was doing. Constantine climbed on top of one of the elegant statues and made himself at home, which also gave him a good vantage point in case those two cowards betrayed him.

"Anubis, can you hear me?" Constantine asked through his mind, trying to keep his tone normal. He didn't want to keep shouting with his thoughts.

"Of course, I can. Who else do you talk to with your thoughts?" Anubis replied, a hint of amusement in his voice.

"What are you doing?" Constantine asked just as he spied a group of cats darting outside the temple. This was better than expected. He hadn't thought the cats would activate their network, but now that they had, it made things much easier.

"I'm napping on this weird, suspended bed the priest installed for me," Anubis answered.

"I have no idea what you are talking about," Constantine admitted.

"It's hard to explain. It looks like a giant sheet, but instead of being flat on the ground, it's attached to two columns. Oh, and it sways. Now I just need the people with the leaves to fan me and I would look like royalty." He laughed at his own joke.

"Why do you need a floating bed when you don't sleep?" Constantine asked Anubis.

"Why do you have to rain on my parade by shooting facts at me?" Anubis answered. Constantine slapped his head with his paw. He was sure Anubis had lost his mind with this whole temple situation. "Besides, it is not my fault this priest keeps bringing chairs and beds to my shrine," Anubis added.

"That is weird. You don't sit or lay. Those are totally useless things for you." It honestly made Constantine question how smart Anubis's priests were.

"Maybe I should ask for a chariot." Anubis sounded giddy at the idea.

"You don't ride, remember? You magically appear everywhere you go." Constantine was on a roll. Gods did not live in the same reality as the rest of them.

"I hate when you are right," Anubis admitted after a while. "Maybe I need a leaning thing."

Constantine paused. He had no idea what he was talking about, so he said, "I have no idea what that might be."

"You know, something that I can lean on every time I arrive somewhere so I can look regal," Anubis said. By the tone of his voice, he was serious, too.

"You want them to build you a moveable wall?" That was the first thing that came to Constantine's mind.

"Of course not. I don't want a wall, although it does fit my needs," Anubis conceded. "What have you been doing besides collecting sick human families?"

"Oh, the usual. Sitting on top of Ptah's statue waiting for his spies to come back with information," Constantine replied in a mocking tone.

"Constantine, do not destroy that statue. Even better, get off it." Anubis's tone turned high-pitched and was filled with alarm.

"Relax. I'm not planning on destroying the temple. Just patiently waiting," Constantine said as calmly as possible.

"How did you manage to get those pesky cats to help you? They don't even help Ptah," Anubis asked, a little calmer now.

"It seems when you slap your biggest adversary across the marketplace, word spreads around the city," Constantine told him with a smile on his face. "All the corrupt Alphas of the city are running scared. They think I'm back for revenge and with a god to back me up." He licked his paw lazily.

"They are not technically wrong. You *are* out for revenge and *do* have a god backing you," Anubis told Constantine. "Have you told them it's not them you want revenge from?"

"And lose the opportunity to instill fear in their souls? Never." Constantine snickered. "Maybe they will learn how to treat the common cats by the time I'm through."

"I doubt it. They will just fear you and still be terrible to all the other cats," Anubis said in his calm voice.

"Well, at least they will fear someone." Constantine did not like this alternative, but at least it was a start.

"So, are your friends helping us?" Anubis changed the subject again.

"Absolutely. After your great display of power, the family is in," Constantine said as he stopped moving to watch the cats outside running everywhere. He wondered what orders those two silly cats had given them.

"What's the plan?" Anubis asked.

"Right now, everyone is looking for our thieves. Once we find them, we will reclaim our property. I'm still working on the rest." Constantine realized his plan had a few holes, but they would come together. At least that was his hope.

"Oh, I must go," Anubis told Constantine. "The priests are burning some weird herbs again. I need to find a way to stop them. Those things are horrible."

"Good luck," Constantine told Anubis. Without a response, Anubis was gone.

Constantine decided he had wasted enough time. He needed to get back to the house and see if the boys had found anything. He didn't trust the temple cats, so he was going to wait for them to clear out before leaving.

Chapter Eight

Constantine made his way back to Ammon's house at a much slower pace. He was no longer hiding in the shadows, instead strolling down the middle of the street like a conqueror. The bullying cats around the area avoided him, but the little ones he had helped followed him in silence. In less than a full day, Constantine was the undisputed king of the cats. Even the other animals noticed his presence.

By the time he made it to the house, the place was busting with excitement. The boys were back and they brought two more kids with them. Constantine wasn't sure how he felt about all these people being around him. He enjoyed people, just not huge crowds of them.

As he walked inside, Ammon was the first to notice him. "We found them. They are in the city."

"Slow down, now," Constantine told Ammon as he moved further inside.

The humans were crowded around him and he hated having to look all the way up to see them. Constantine knew that humans told a lot more of their intentions with their facial movements than their words. He didn't want to miss a single detail now that he could communicate with them. He quickly jumped on the table for a better angle.

"Now, start from the beginning," Constantine told the group.

"We didn't think it was going to be this easy," Pilis told him. "The artisans' shops are packed with people talking about the weird events at Saqqara. It seems the priests have been lacking in their duties and Anubis is punishing them. He sent his messenger to torment them at night." Pilis looked at Constantine for confirmation.

"I did not torment any of the priests," Constantine defended. "It is not my fault they don't listen and jumped to conclusions." He sat down on the table, looking as dignified as only a cat could. He tucked his legs underneath him and straightened his back.

"Well, the news spread across the working artisans and they all left in the middle of the night," Ammon jumped in. "The foremen are recruiting new workers."

"Are many people signing up?" Constantine asked, looking at Ammon closely.

"That's the best part: everyone is scared," Pilis told them with a huge grin on his face.

"We must have a different meaning for the word 'best.' How is that a good thing, again?" Constantine asked the boy, narrowing his eyes. Maybe the kid had hit his head too many times or something.

"Simple. They are desperate and accepting anyone who signs up," Ammon explained. "We both did and so did the brothers." He pointed to the other two boys near the kitchen area.

The two boys were around the same age as Ammon, and not yet to manhood. They were thinner and looked like they missed too many meals. Ammon's mom was busy making them food. Constantine figured this was the house where all the orphans came for aid. Before long, the boys shoveled food into their mouths, and it made Constantine grateful that Anubis had packed such a large sack for them.

"Are you sure you all want to go to Saqqara?" he asked, wanting them to go, but not wanting anyone to go who was afraid.

"Of course, we will," Pilis told him. "This could be the only way to get those thieves."

"In that case, pack some clothes. The crew for Saqqara is usually away for seven sun downs," Constantine told the boys.

"That is easy. There isn't much to pack besides the clothes on our backs," Ammon told Constantine. There wasn't pity in his voice, only the strength of a man that had been through too much too soon. The boys might be young in body, but life had dealt them a rough hand.

Before Constantine could say anything, a light knock came from the door. The boys froze, and their eyes darted nervously to each other.

"Meow," the soft sound came from the other side of the door.

"Oh, that's for me," Constantine told the boys as he jumped off the table.

Ammon walked with Constantine and opened the door for him. Outside, a scrawny little cat stood by the corner. He had twitchy little eyes and was missing patches of fur. Constantine had never seen him before, but knew he was one of the dock cats. He reeked of fish. In fact, Constantine thought he looked more like a large rat. What a disgrace!

"Yes?" Constantine asked, staring at the little cat.

"Master Constantine, we found them," the little cat told him, looking around the street carefully.

"Good. Wait here," Constantine told the cat right before he turned around.

"What did he say?" Ammon asked while everyone stared in their direction.

"They found the house where the foremen are hiding," Constantine told them. "I need to check if they brought back the goods they stole from the temple. If they did, we are taking it back." The last part came out in a cold voice.

"Are we coming with you?" Pilis said, almost bouncing on the balls of his feet.

"No," Constantine said, and the boys looked like they were going to cry. "Four human boys wandering the city at this time would look suspicious. Wait here. Once we have secured the goods, I'll send for you." First, he had to figure out how he would be able to do that.

"I'll do it," Moses told him, squeezing between Ammon and Pilis.

The boys looked down at their little kitten, trying to figure out what was going on.

"Perfect," Constantine told the group. "Moses will come with us. As soon as we have the house secure, he will come and get you."

"Is that safe?" Ammon asked, bending down to pet his little kitten.

"Don't underestimate him. Moses is tougher than he looks," Constantine told Ammon, making Moses puff out with pride.

"Constantine is right, my son, Moses can handle it," Ammon's mother added.

"It is going to be a long night. Stay alert," Constantine told the boys. "Ready, Moses?"

"Ready, boss," the little kitten replied.

"Okay, rat boy, lead the way," Constantine told the beat-down cat waiting outside. "But remember, if this is a trap, I will send each and every one of you straight to the underworld. Is that clear?" His sharp claws were out and pointed at the scrawny cat for extra emphasis.

"We will never betray you, Master Constantine," the scrawny cat said as he pushed away from Constantine.

"Good, go," Constantine told the cat.

To Moses, Constantine said, "Keep your eyes open, Moses. This could get ugly." And then, he took off after the scrawny cat.

Chapter Nine

I f the scrawny cat was taking them to the correct location, Constantine figured the thieves were hiding in the fishermen's quarters. Also, it would explain why this little fellow brought the news. The humans in the city followed a very distinct schedule. By the time night came, most of them were asleep to avoid wasting candles and supplies. This meant that besides the guards patrolling the city, the place belonged to the cats.

When they reached the fishermen's quarters, Constantine stayed alert. A few men stumbled around, probably heading home for the night. There had been talk of a few night crews that only fished late at night, but Constantine had never seen it until now. Although, he had to admit he had admiration for them since they knew the meaning of dedication.

The house the scrawny cat led him to was nothing to brag about. With all the loot the thieves had taken, Constantine expected them to be living a grand life, but their house was not much bigger than Ammon's.

"Are you sure this is the right place?" Constantine asked the little fellow.

"This is it." He wouldn't make eye contact. "We searched everyone to make sure it's the right one."

"Do you know who is in the house?" Constantine could hear voices, but he had to make sure how many people were inside. There was no point in going into a fight blind.

"Meow!" the scrawny cat let out a loud scream.

"Oh, thank you." Constantine held his paws over his ears. "I needed to lose my hearing today."

Two cats dropped down from the roof of the house. They looked just as rough as the first one. The first cat had deep-black fur, while the other one was a golden-brown. Constantine was sure in another life they had been handsome fellows.

"Are they here?" asked Scrawny.

"Three men and two women," the black one replied.

"How do so many people fit in such little spaces?" Constantine asked, more to himself than the others. "Do they all live there?"

"Only the two you are looking for," the black one replied, almost hissing. "The women are port walkers and the other man is one of their workers."

Loud shouting and cheering erupted from inside, pulling their gazes towards the place.

"We need to find out if they brought the goods from the temple here," Constantine told the group as he examined the layout of the little house.

"The back room is filled with human junk," the brown cat told them.

"Are you sure?" Constantine asked as he moved closer.

"There is a window on that side." A mischievous glint shone from the brown cat's eyes.

"Do they have food in the house?" Constantine asked the cats as a crazy plan developed in his mind.

"It's loaded." The black cat licked his mouth.

"How about we make a deal?" Constantine told the cats. "Help me get rid of the humans and get my goods back, and you can have all the food you find in the house." Constantine knew the power of hunger and the three cats in front of him looked like they were starving.

"You two won't take any?" the scrawny one asked, eyeing Constantine and Moses.

"The food is all yours," Constantine told them. "We just want the goods."

"Well, Master Constantine, it seems the rumors were right. You are nothing like those arrogant cats in power," Scrawny told Constantine with a smile. "Welcome to the fishermen's party. We are here to serve." He bowed his head to Constantine, and the other two followed.

"Then we have a deal." Constantine bowed back to them. "Moses, get the boys. By the time you get back, we should be all done."

"Yes, Constantine," Moses replied and took off back to his side of town.

"Boys, you know what to do," Scrawny told the other two cats, and they immediately ran off in opposite directions.

"Are they coming back?" Constantine asked as he watched the two cats running.

"They are getting the rest of the troops. Come on, let's go check out your treasure." Scrawny stepped towards the back of the house. With no other option, Constantine followed closely behind.

Constantine was starting to wonder how many crazy cats lived in this city. It was a blessing the Egyptians worshipped cats, or all these nuts would have been dead by now.

Scrawny stopped in front of a small window in the back of the house. The window was pretty high from the ground, probably to discourage humans from trying to break in. Scrawny scurried up the side of some huge water jugs, around a funny-looking tree, and then somersaulted towards the window.

Constantine jutted his bottom lip out and nodded his head, impressed, but he was way too lazy to do all that for one window. Instead, he angled himself in front of it and bent down, then he sprung into a huge leap. He easily made the jump and landed next to Scrawny.

Scrawny looked closely at Constantine and then down at the floor. "I don't want to know how you managed that. Even our best jumpers can't reach this height." His eyes took in Constantine, all of him.

"Divine intervention?" Constantine shrugged. "Best not to think too hard on it." He gave Scrawny one last look before jumping inside the house.

Scrawny shadowed Constantine and smacked right into him when Constantine stopped abruptly. He took in the room they had entered. It was poor for human standards, with pointless objects piled up around the filth. Luckily, cats had no issues navigating in the dark, and he found the sacks filled with temple items in a flash. That wasn't all he found, though. There were other sacks stuffed to the brim with jewels, and from the looks of them, they came from Ptah's temple.

"It seems our little friends made their rounds around town," Constantine told Scrawny, pointing to all the sacks.

"What do you want to do?" Scrawny asked.

"We take it all. I'm sure Anubis can find a way to return it to the right temple," Constantine answered as another cat landed in the room with them.

"All it is, then," Scrawny replied, licking his mouth.

Constantine's stomach dropped. He had a feeling the little cat needed food, and some healing for that matter. Maybe there would be time after they finished their mission.

"Fury, to the front door. Get the other ones in," Scrawny told the new arrival.

Constantine had no clue why they called him Fury, although maybe it had something to do with his dark-orange fur. A rare breed in these parts.

Fury slithered out of the room, almost like a snake. Constantine and Scrawny followed him to the doorway, where the door was missing. The only thing separating it was a thin sheet. The cats peered through the sheet and watched Fury maneuver around the humans, working his way toward the front door. When he reached it, he used his front paws to knock as loud as he could.

What was the point of that, Constantine thought. But he understood when one of the humans went to the door and opened it, letting in a group of cats.

"Who is at the door?" one of the humans yelled.

"Nobody," the man at the door replied, scratching his head. "Maybe I'm hearing things."

"Leave the door and come here," one of the women said to the man. The man smiled, turned, and shoved the door, but Fury stood in the middle, ensuring it didn't shut all the way.

Constantine waited while more cats joined the group. Some came in from the small space in the front door, and others from the windows in the house. Constantine didn't have time to finish counting how many cats had entered before Scrawny let out a loud whistle.

Chaos erupted. Everywhere. Cats flew at the humans from every angle, and any object not nailed down was tossed in the air.

"Are you coming?" Scrawny asked Constantine as he rushed to join the fun.

"I wouldn't miss it for the world," Constantine said. "I have a score to settle."

The cats were destroying everything. In their distress, the humans flipped over a table and knocked down chairs, creating a sort of barrier for them to hide behind. As Constantine came closer, though, he realized they hadn't hidden fast enough. Both females' clothes had been scratched to shreds.

The barrier didn't hide them for long, and soon the cats swarmed two of the men, biting and scratching them everywhere. Constantine found the shorter of the two robbers, who had backed against a wall as a form of protection against the four cats assaulting him.

"Get away from me!" the short robber screamed.

"I told you the gods were going to punish us," the tall robber yelled from behind the table where he was hiding again.

"Oh, trust me, you will pay," Constantine told them as he strolled towards the men with a predatory sway.

"He is back from the dead!" the tall one screamed right before he crawled out the door. He moved so fast that Constantine couldn't figure out how he did it. He had never seen a human move so fast while on his knees. Fear must be a powerful motivator.

"Time to die." Constantine growled, and the other cats joined in, creating an orchestra of menacing quality.

"Somebody! Please, save us!" screamed the women, who pushed their way out of the house.

Left alone, the short thief lost his bravery and took off, too, leaving their friend behind. He couldn't get up, but he swung his arms around—like that would help him. Fear lined every feature on his face as six cats clawed his pants, which were around his ankles.

Constantine shook his head. He didn't want to know why his pants were down.

"Knock him out," Constantine demanded.

"With pleasure," the six cats replied at once.

The angry cat dropped a flower basin on top of the man's head. Shards of clay went flying, but it stopped the man from moving around like a dead snake.

The cats didn't waste any time. Once the man was unconscious, a large group dragged him out of the house.

"Nice work everyone," Constantine told the fishermen's party.

"This was fun," one of the cats by the window told them.

"We don't have a lot of time before the humans come to check the area. Grab all the food and leave," Scrawny told his pack.

Constantine watched as a cyclone of fur moved through the house. He shifted as far away as he could from the main room so he wouldn't be knocked down.

"Do you need us to wait with you?" Scrawny asked Constantine, who was now staring out the door.

"I think my group just arrived," Constantine told Scrawny as he spotted Moses and the boys heading their way. "But, could you help us get to the edge of the city? I got some friends I need to meet."

"It would be our pleasure," Scrawny told Constantine with a wicked grin. "Fury, Chaos, with me," Scrawny said, and the three cats disappeared into the night.

"Constantine, we are here," Ammon said, a little out of breath. He picked up Moses and put him on his shoulder. The poor kitten looked exhausted.

"Hurry, we don't have a lot of time. Go to the back room and grab all the sacks you can, then follow me."

The boys didn't ask any questions. They rushed to the back, bragging about which could carry more sacks. Either way, Constantine was proud. Not a single sack was left behind.

"Remind me to never make a cat mad," Pilis told Ammon.

"Oh, trust me, I won't ever make that mistake," Ammon replied in a soft voice.

"Ready?" Constantine whispered and both boys nodded. "We are ready," Constantine said to the shadows.

With his enhanced vision, Constantine saw Scrawny and Fury on the rooftops. Each cat bowed their heads at him before they took off.

"Follow me very closely," Constantine said before he rushed toward the other cats.

Constantine wasn't too familiar with this side of the city. The houses were not impressive, all made from the same type of mud material, but the air carried the scent of the Nile and palm trees were more prominent. If the fishermen's party weren't such a nutty group of cats, this would be a great place to live.

Scrawny did not disappoint. After a few weird turns and near misses with the guards, he guided them to the edge of the city.

"How exactly are you planning to cross that?" Scrawny asked Constantine as he glanced at the immense desert.

"I got friends," Constantine told him and walked a little further ahead of the group. He let out a loud whistle and waited.

"What are we doing here?" Ammon asked, looking around the desert and at his friends.

"You will see," Constantine said softly.

From the shadows of the desert, the pack of jackals appeared.

"We are dead," mumbled Pilis.

"The human is right," added Fury.

"Enough," Constantine told them and walked over to meet the Alpha.

The female Alpha bowed her head and Constantine did the same.

"Is the offer for a guide still available?" Constantine asked her.

"Of course, my master," she replied, licking her lips and staring at the group by the edge with hungry eyes.

"Sorry, they are not lunch. I'll owe you dinner at Saqqara," Constantine told her before the pack moved in. "I do need some help carrying the sacks." He gave her a wolfish grin.

"You ask a lot, Constantine," the female replied.

"I know, but I'm irresistible," Constantine told her and the female just shook her head.

"Let's make this quick. We need to be at Saqqara before dawn." She signaled her pack to follow.

The kids and the cats were ready to bolt. "Relax, they are with me!" Constantine yelled before they could run.

"You keep strange company," Fury told Constantine.

"It's probably because I'm the only one everyone can understand." Constantine rubbed his face. "Okay, guys, please give the sacks to the jackals," he told them. "Jackals, please don't eat them. I need them tomorrow."

The jackals only glared at Constantine. In the end, though, they all gave a subtle nod.

The transfer went as smoothly as possible. All the jackals carried a bag, leaving one left over. Nobody made any sudden movements. Instead, they all remained as still as possible.

"Constantine, what should we do with this one?" Ammon asked, holding the last sack up.

"I'll take that one," Constantine told him.

"How?" asked Pilis.

"My turn," Constantine told the crowd as he closed his eyes.

Become a jackal, Constantine told himself. With those simple words, his body shifted. By the time he opened his eyes, he had changed.

"I'll take that," Constantine told the group, and when his eyes landed on them, their mouths were all hanging open. "Ammon, I'll see your team in the morning at Saqqara."

"Yes, Constantine," Ammon replied, bowing in front of him. The other boys followed suit, and even Moses joined in.

"Fishermen, thank you. I will never forget this," Constantine told the three cats.

"It was our honor, Master Constantine. Join us again," Scrawny replied and the cats also bowed before him.

Constantine was really enjoying this new turn of events. Grabbing the sack, he headed toward the jackals.

"Welcome back, Constantine," the female Alpha told him, and then they took off.

Even with the heavy sack, Constantine felt free and alive.

Chapter Ten

T he jackals and Constantine made it to Saqqara as dawn was approaching. Anubis waited at the edge of the Necropolis, sitting on some strange contraption. As Constantine approached, he noticed Anubis was also drinking from a coconut. The jackals slowed down and stopped in front of Anubis, who put his drink down and stood to meet them.

"It seems your adventures went well," Anubis told Constantine, looking at all the sacks. "I didn't think they took that much stuff." Anubis walked over to the jackals and examined the goods.

Constantine dropped his sack so he could talk. "They didn't, at least not from us. I think they stole the rest from your other god friends," he told him as Anubis picked up a small statue.

"You are right," Anubis said. "Only Ptah's people would make such hideous looking things and call it art." He dropped the statue back in the sack.

"Do you mind feeding my friends? It was a long journey," Constantine asked Anubis on behalf of the jackals.

"Of course," Anubis told him and snapped his fingers. Two large cows appeared not too far from the group.

"Thank you, Constantine," the Alpha told Constantine.

"Don't thank me; thank Anubis. He is the one with the magic," Constantine said.

"Thank you, my Lord," she told the god.

"Enjoy," Anubis told her and the jackals took off.

"I don't think your cow goddess is going to be very happy with you," Constantine told Anubis as he shifted back to his normal body.

"Hey, it's as fresh as it gets, and it was the first thing that popped in my head that would feed so many hungry jackals." Anubis headed back to his chair to avoid watching the feeding frenzy.

"By the way, what are you drinking? And where did you find that thing?" Constantine asked Anubis as he pointed to the funny looking chair.

"In one of my travels, I saw one and couldn't resist." Anubis rubbed his chair with pride. "And the priests left all these coconuts in the temple. They are surprisingly refreshing once you get inside of them." He took another drink.

"Once again, you don't even drink. Why are you doing all this?" Constantine asked Anubis as he smelled the coconut.

Before Anubis could reply, the head priest and his assistant rushed at them.

"Oh, my Lord, forgive us." The two men bowed in front of Constantine and not Anubis.

"I'm confused," Constantine told Anubis.

"What is wrong with these fools? Why can't they ever see me?" Anubis shouted at the priests.

"Maybe you should concentrate a little harder so they can see you," Constantine told Anubis in his mind.

"Please have mercy on us," the head priest begged.

"You do know I'm not Anubis?" Constantine asked the two men.

"Yes, but you are his messenger. We are not worthy to see the god ourselves," the head priest told Constantine.

"Well, that explains it. They don't think they should see you, so they don't," Constantine told Anubis in his mind.

"Humans are idiots!" Anubis screamed and rushed at the head priest. He grabbed him by the head and stared down at him. "Can you see me now?" Anubis screamed at the priest as he held him.

The priest screamed so loud, the jackals turned around.

"Don't mind him, he is fine," Constantine told the group and they went back to eating. By the time Constantine turned around, the priest had passed out.

"That is not going to help us," Constantine told Anubis.

Anubis dropped the priest and turned around. "Fine, you talk to them. I'm going inside to nap." Right as his bottom lip poked out, he disappeared.

"It's going to be a long day," Constantine mumbled to himself. Then he turned to face the assistant, who was puking on the sand.

"Lord Anubis is angry with us. We are all going to die." The poor man was rambling, and he had drool running down his chin. It was a horrible sight, even for Constantine.

"Man, pull yourself together," Constantine told the assistant as he walked over. "Anubis is not mad at you, but he is upset." He decided to take this opportunity to bring the priests to his side. "Terrible men violated the sanctity of Anubis's temple, they stole from him and are coming back to finish the job. It is our job to stop them. Do you understand me?"

"Yes, Master," the assistant replied, his eyes wide and his facial color changing to an ugly yellow. Constantine wondered how humans survived so many emotions when their reactions were so drastic.

"The thieves could be coming back at any moment. We need to be ready. I have a few friends who will be helping us. We don't have a lot of time, so we need to prepare a few surprises for our guests."

"So, the god Anubis is not going to punish us?" the assistant asked, still focused on his punishment. At least his breathing had returned to normal, though.

"No, unless you don't do as I say and help us catch the criminals. Is that clear?" Constantine growled the last part.

"Yes, Master," the assistant said, bowing again.

Annoyance clouded Constantine's features. Why did he have to shout at these humans to get them to follow simple instructions?

"Take these sacks inside and hide them. Also, make sure none of the other priests speak with the work crew. We don't want them to give away our secret," Constantine told the assistant. "Once you have gathered the sacks, get everyone to the temple. We need to plan."

Constantine took off before the man could answer. Hopefully, those men were amazing priests, because they were pretty useless for everything else. He needed to formulate a plan quickly, check on Anubis, and clean himself off. His fur was not as shiny as it should be. Fixing the world was really time consuming. He hadn't had a nap in days.

The workers were late arriving. Maybe Constantine had scared the robbers so badly that they decided not to come, which wouldn't be a bad thing. Except the two thieves would get off scot-free. If left to roam, Constantine had a feeling they would just find another temple to vandalize.

Constantine paced by the door of the temple, unable to calm down.

"If you keep that up, you are going to wear a hole in the stone," Anubis told him from behind.

"I thought you didn't care about it," Constantine told Anubis.

Anubis shrugged. "I care."

"So, you are just jealous your priests are talking to me?" Constantine asked, not looking at the god.

"I'm sorry, Constantine. It's not your fault."

"I know it's not my fault," Constantine growled at Anubis.

"This is not working out too well." Anubis paused and shook his head. "What I mean to say is, nobody sees me because of *me*." His tone was weak, sad.

"Explain," Constantine said in a softer voice.

"I have been so busy following the rules and not getting involved in the affairs of humans that my own priests don't recognize me," Anubis told him, his voice cracking. "I made myself invisible." He dropped down on the floor.

Constantine walked over to him and sat down. "You can change that if you want," he told him. "Ammon and his family saw you. So, others could see you, too." He put his paw on Anubis's arm.

"They saw a healer, not Anubis," Anubis corrected, his eyes brimming with unshed tears.

"That is crazy." Constantine shook his head. "They saw *you*. They knew who you were. Besides, when you are angry, you have no problems making yourself be seen. So, stop this. You can do whatever you want."

"For a little cat, you really are wise." Anubis rubbed Constantine's ears.

"And handsome, so stop messing up the fur," Constantine told him as he playfully slapped his hand away.

"Your friends are here," Anubis told Constantine.

"Really?" Constantine ran to the door to check. Anubis was right. The workers had arrived, including his friends and those two pesky thieves. "You are good." He turned to tell Anubis, but he was gone. "What am I going to do with that god?"

That was a question for another time, though. He needed to make contact with his friends without being seen by the foremen. Constantine tracked the foremen to the edge of the group. They looked horrible. Scrawny's cats had not been playing with those two, which made him wonder if the foremen had done something to the cats before this.

The head priest hobbled over to give instructions to the workers. From Constantine's location, the poor man looked like only bones.

The workers dispersed to their designated locations. Constantine decided to follow the two foremen. They walked slowly behind the temple to the supply shed. Constantine crawled, making sure he stayed a safe distance away so they couldn't see him. He decided to use his enhanced hearing to eavesdrop on the conversation. It took him a minute to figure out how, but once he was able to concentrate on the two men and tune every other noise out, it worked.

"We shouldn't be here," the tall man said. "After last night, we should have left the city." He looked over his shoulder, shaking.

"With what?" the short one said sharply. "We lost everything. We need this." He pointed at the temple as he spoke.

"This place is haunted by that cat you killed," the tall one whispered. "You saw him. He came back from the underworld to hunt us." The tall man tried to grab a bucket from the supply cart, but couldn't hold on to it.

"You need to calm down and focus. You will attract attention to us," the short man said as he grabbed the tall one by his tunic. "We go in tonight, take everything, and then we disappear. Got it?"

The tall man was shaking so badly, it looked like he couldn't talk, so he just nodded.

Constantine had all the information he needed. He headed across the field to find his friends. Normally, the workers set up their tents before staring to work. The tent area was near the orchard and not that far from the temple. Constantine did not want anyone to notice him, so he clung to the shadows.

The boys were putting up a tent, but they were having issues. Luckily, the older boys were helping them, but that meant Constantine had to wait until they left, so he made himself comfortable by a fruit tree and waited.

Constantine never thought setting up a tent would be so complicated, but it felt like an eternity before they finished. Once they did and the older boys retreated, Constantine snuck in through the back. He found the boys rolling out their beds.

"That looked like a painful process," Constantine told them.

"It was," Pilis admitted.

"Our group leader felt bad, so he volunteered to help. But he had never set one up on his own," Ammon explained. "So, nothing he suggested worked." He dropped to the ground. "How are you doing?" Ammon asked Constantine.

"In a surprising turn of events, the priests are helping us," Constantine told them with a grin.

"That is great," one of the two silent boys said, surprising Constantine. He had thought they were mutes.

"Do you still need us?" Pilis asked.

"Well, the priests are great for planning, but horrible for manual labor," Constantine explained. "But, I heard our favorite thieves discussing their plans. They are preparing to take everything today. We have traps set up in the temple, but we need you to activate them."

"Don't worry, Constantine. We told you we would help, and we will," Ammon reassured him. "What time are we meeting?"

"We all must be in position in the temple room before sundown. I doubt they'll make their move much later than that. Just remember, they are desperate and dangerous," Constantine told the boys. Then he reflected on his own choices. Should he have involved the boys when they were only kids? It was too late now, but he hoped nothing happened to them or he would never forgive himself.

He couldn't turn back now. The decisions had been made. Everything was in motion. And there was no way he would allow the thieves to desecrate Anubis's temple again.

"You can count on us, Constantine," Pilis told him.

"We better hurry before anyone notices we are missing," Ammon added. The boys nodded, then they left the tent in a hurry.

Constantine decided to spend the day spying on the foremen and making sure they didn't change their plans. He left the tent the same way he came in and retraced his steps.

Chapter Eleven

E verything was set. The traps were in place, the boys were in their designated locations, and the priests were pretending to head to bed early to be ready for their early morning prayers. All Constantine needed to do was wait—something he had gotten really good at. Since Anubis was nowhere to be found, Constantine got comfortable in one of his new lounging chairs. He'd been right, too. They were comfortable, and the temple was filled with furniture of all kinds. Did they honestly believe all gods did was lay around? Maybe some, but definitely not Anubis.

The temple area was dark, so it was Constantine's job to warn everyone when the pair arrived. He had started dozing off when he finally heard them, so he jumped up and snuck to the temple area to watch. Both thieves were back, ambling around in the dark.

"Wake up, everyone! They are coming!" Constantine whisper-yelled.

Constantine made his way to the back of the room, stopping at every boy to make sure they heard him. Ammon and Pilis were in charge of dropping the net as soon as the thieves grabbed the goods. The other two would block off the door and sound the alarm. It was a simple but elegant plan.

The foremen made it to the temple area and lit a candle once they were inside. After the overwhelming darkness, the little candle looked like the sun shining in the room. Constantine's eyes adjusted quickly, but he noticed the boys weren't having the same luck. It left

Pilis in plain view, and the short man noticed before Constantine could do a thing about it.

"What do we have here? A thief?" the short man told Pilis as he grabbed him by his tunic.

"Let go of me!" Pilis jerked and squirmed, trying to free himself, but in the end he couldn't.

"What are we going to do?" the tall man ran over to them, his voice panicked.

"We are going to get a reward. Wait until the priests find out we caught a thief in their chamber as we were making our last-minute rounds," the short man said. "Our luck is improving. You will be dead before dawn." The last part was directed at Pilis, who was trying to get away.

"Let him go!" Ammon screamed as he charged at the two men. He was quickly stopped by the tall one, who slammed him against a wall, knocking him out.

This is not going according to plan, Constantine told himself. *How can a bunch of cats take these two men out, but human boys are struggling?*

The other two boys charged, and were instantly snatched up.

"This is better than I expected. Hurry, pack the sacks. We will blame the looting on these four and watch them hang." The tall man followed the instructions and started packing the sacks, but the short man turned back to Pilis. "Why wait until tomorrow? We will kill you now and there will be no witnesses." the short man wrapped his hands around Pilis's neck, squeezing.

Constantine was running out of time and his plan had fallen apart in less than three blinks. He couldn't let the boys die because of him. He leapt from his hiding spot, landing in front of the short man.

"Drop the boy before I rip your throat apart!" Constantine growled at the man.

"No! He is back!" the tall man screamed. "He is guarding the underworld and we are trespassing."

Constantine shook his head. Did every human jump to conclusions so quickly, or was it just the one standing before him?

"What are you going to do, little cat?" the short man teased, lowering Pilis and releasing his hold on his neck. "You are not so tough without your pack of wild cats."

Constantine only smiled at the man and willed himself to shift. This time he chose a lion instead of a jackal. The process was getting easier and faster.

"How do you like me now?" Constantine growled.

The tall man's shrill scream rent the air. Then he shouted, "We are dead!"

"Put the boy down and turn yourself in." Constantine's voice was deadly soft.

"Never," the short man told him as he pulled a knife from an inside pocket and placed it next to Pilis's neck.

Constantine was afraid to move. If he attacked them, Pilis would die. Were the boys' lives worth more any of the stuff in this room? Constantine knew they were, so he slowly backed away, but he didn't stop growling at them.

"That's a good, little cat. You are going to watch us take all of Anubis's toys and there is nothing you can do about it." The short man laughed.

"You should have listened to my friend." Anubis appeared behind the men in full battle armor. His eyes glowed red and steam came from his mouth.

Anubis lifted the short man off the ground and ripped Pilis from him, dropping him a safe distance away.

Constantine didn't know how angry Anubis was, so he moved away, too. Just in case.

The tall man tried to run, but Anubis grabbed him by his shirt and yanked him back.

"So, you don't believe in gods? Sounds like I need to teach you a lesson," Anubis told the two men as they started to scream.

Ammon woke up just in time to watch the God of Death disappear with the two thieves into nothingness. Constantine wasn't sure what to do, so he shifted back to his normal self.

"What just happened?" Ammon asked.

"I don't think we want to know," Constantine answered.

Poor Pilis was on the ground unconscious when the priests rushed in yelling. They were carrying sticks and a broom.

"Release them!" the head priest shouted.

When they entered the room, their eyes fell on Constantine and the beat-down boys, making them stop short.

"Where are the thieves?" the assistant asked, looking around the room.

"Oh, don't worry, Anubis took care of them," Constantine told the men, and each one of them turned pale.

"What's going to happen to them?" Ammon asked as he helped Pilis stand.

"I don't think we are supposed to know, even if we wanted to," Constantine said in a gentle tone. "But I'm so glad you all made it here and I didn't have to find you," he told the priests in a no-nonsense voice. "These kids need food, healing, and sleep. They were injured defending your god, so the least you can do is take care of them. What are you waiting for? Go!"

They rushed forward after a moment's hesitation, and Constantine had to stifle a laugh. He really was getting good at this.

"What are you going to do, Master Constantine?" the assistant asked after all the priests had left the chamber with the boys.

"I'll wait for Anubis. I'm sure he will be back soon," Constantine told the man, hoping he was right

Anubis didn't return that night. It was a full week before he came back. Constantine was sitting in Anubis's favorite corner when he came. When the god sat next to Constantine, the cat moved closer to him.

"I was afraid you wouldn't come back," Constantine whispered.

"I won't be staying," Anubis replied. "How are the boys?"

"Well. The priests have taken them in, and Ammon's family, too." Constantine didn't meet Anubis's eyes. "After the foremen vanished, the rest of the workers got scared and left. The only ones that wanted to stay were the boys. You now have a new group of priests in training and they are all ready to worship you," Constantine said, trying to smile. "What happened to the thieves?"

"I delivered them to a few gods who don't enjoy people stealing from them," Anubis said. "Rumors are spreading through Memphis of how adored you are. How does it feel?" Anubis looked at the floor.

"Lonely. The world fears me now," Constantine told him honestly.

"I'm leaving," Anubis said. "Egypt is not for me. There is a huge world with other people to explore. I'm tired of being a god."

"What will you be, then?" Constantine asked, this time looking at his friend with misty eyes.

"Death, the companion of souls," Anubis whispered. "You know you can always reach me, right?" he asked, barely audible.

"I know," Constantine replied.

The two sat in awkward silence.

"What will you do?" Anubis asked, staring at the walls.

"I don't know," Constantine said. "Maybe I can join the jackals, run away."

"Really?" Anubis asked, his voice echoing in the chamber.

"I'm not too crazy about humans," Constantine admitted. Anubis laughed. "What is so funny?"

"I thought you couldn't wait to be worshipped and adored," Anubis said with a huge grin.

"They are driving me insane with all their never-ending questions," Constantine hissed.

"Join me," Anubis told him.

"Are you sure? I didn't think you wanted me to," Constantine said, sitting up for the first time.

"I didn't want you to come with me out of duty or pity. We won't be living here again, Constantine. The world will be our home," Anubis said.

"That is the best news I've heard today. Let's go. I'm ready," Constantine told the former god.

"Don't you want to say goodbye?" Anubis asked softly.

"I already did. I was just waiting for you to come back," Constantine answered with a smile. "But if we are leaving Egypt, you might need to lose the head. You won't blend in very well outside of here." Constantine pointed at Anubis's jackal face.

Anubis touched his face and closed his eyes. His features shifted and the handsome young man with the bright-blue eyes was back.

"Ready, my friend?" Anubis asked.

"Always," Constantine replied.

Anubis picked him up and placed him around his shoulders.

"Freedom!" Constantine shouted.

"To freedom!" Anubis echoed and they vanished from Egypt.

Chapter Twelve

P resent day–Texarkana
Bob stared at Constantine with his mouth hanging open. Constantine finally looked his way.

"Bob, didn't I tell you to close your mouth before a fly gets in there," Constantine said.

"Sorry, boss," Bob answered. "That is just amazing."

"I could be a little fuzzy on the details. It was five thousand years ago," Constantine told Bob as he licked his paws and wiped his face. "I'm technically the original ride or die." He gave Bob a huge grin

"That might be an understatement," Bob said as he scanned the street one more time. "Boss, so you basically have been instigating riots and chaos for a millennium. Do you miss it?" Bob turned, meeting Constantine's eyes.

"I miss the architecture. People don't make things like that anymore." His voice softened as he spoke. "The rest, not so much. The world smells better now. I like that people bathe all the time. Besides, who would keep Death humble?" Constantine told Bob with a huge nod.

"That is a good questions. Who would?" Death asked, standing by the open window beside Constantine.

Bob sucked in a breath. "Oh my God! Death, don't do that." He put a hand on his chest.

"Sorry, Bob. It's a bad habit," Death apologized with a smile.

"Speaking of bad habits, how long have you been eavesdropping?" Constantine asked, glaring at Death.

"Starting with your first beating by the disciplinarians," Death answered as he played with his short, jet-black hair.

Constantine couldn't help it. He smiled. It was just too hard to stay mad at his best friend as he studied the boyish face he knew so well.

"Basically the whole time, thanks." Constantine stuck his tongue out at Death.

"Hey, it's your story and I love hearing it," Death told Constantine. "You don't share that one often."

"Most humans don't want to know," Constantine said.

"Very true," Death conceded.

"Where are you going?" Constantine asked, if only to change the subject.

"Florida. Famine is acting weird, so I'm going to check up on them," Death said, checking his watch. Constantine never understood why he wore one when time never made a difference to him. "He should be home now."

"Are they still running a company?" Constantine asked, his curiosity piqued.

"Of course, and making millions." Death stopped talking and turned to face the road. "Is that Isis over there?" He pointed at the midnight-blue mini-Cooper that was speeding down the road.

"Yep, that's her." Constantine shook his head.

"Constantine, do I want to know what's going on?" Death asked, crossing his arms.

"Not right now. You got places to go and we have a streaker soul to catch," Constantine told Death as Bob started the truck. "I'll see you when you get back. Don't forget the sunscreen. Bob, hurry."

"Bye, Death!" Bob yelled out the window and he pulled out of the parking lot.

Constantine looked at Death as he disappeared, but he didn't miss the smile on Death's face.

"Is Death mad at us?" Bob asked.

"Not at all. Just another day in the life of his Interns. You'd better hurry before Isis gets arrested or loses that soul," Constantine told Bob right before they flew down the road, headed towards Downtown.

The End...for now

My dear friend, this Cat has been out-of-control since day one. Probably the reason we all love him. If you are new to the Intern Diaries
Series, make sure to start the adventure with **Death's Intern.**

Or join the boys in another crazy adventure in **From Eugene with Love.** Sometimes, Isis really does not want to know what the boys do when she is gone.

Acknowledgments

Dear Reader,

When super-beta-reader Mr. J. Patton Tidwell recommended doing an origin story on Constantine, I thought the idea was wild. *Who would want to know about that crazy cat?* Little did I know he was going to steal the show and become one of my favorite characters. I truly hope you enjoy this story as much as I did. One of my greatest honors and pleasures is to create stories. Thank you for giving me an opportunity to be part of your family and welcoming Constantine into your life.

This journey would not be possible without the incredible Gomez Tribe. To my family for never given up on me, to Mr. J. Patton Tidwell for being super-beta-reader, to both Cassandra Fear and Michelle Hoffman for all their work editing my books. Above all, thank you to the Almighty for the gift of this story.

If you enjoy the story, please consider leaving a rating and possibly a short review. Your reviews help others find the books you love.

With love,

D. C.

About Author

D. C. Gomez was born in the Dominican Republic, but grew up in Salem, Massachusetts. She studied film and television at New York University. After college, she joined the US Army, and proudly served for four years.

Those experiences shaped her quirky, and sometimes morbid, sense of humor. D.C. has a love for those who served and the families that support them. She currently lives in the quaint city of Wake Village, Texas, with her furry roommate, Chincha.

Also By D. C. Gomez

In The Reapers' Universe- Urban Fantasy Books

The Intern Diaries Series

Death's Intern- Book 1

Plague Unleashed- Book 2

Forbidden War- Book 3

Unstoppable Famine- Book 4

Judgement Day- Book 5

The Origins of Constantine- Novella

From Eugene with Love- Novella

Rise of the Reapers- Novella

The Order's Assassin Series

The Hitman- Book 1

The Traitor (coming soon)

The Elisha & Elijah Chronicles (UF and Post-Apocalyptic)

Recruited- Book 1

Betrayed- Book 2 (coming soon)

Humorous Fiction

The Cat Lady Special

A Desperate Cat Lady (coming soon)

Young Adult

Another World

Children's Books

Charlie, What's Your Talent? – Book 1

Charlie, Dare to Dream – Book 2

Devotional Books

Dare to Believe

Dare to Forgive

Dare to Love

Made in the USA
Middletown, DE
26 May 2023

30811526R00054